DEATH PACTS

AND

LEFT-HAND PATHS

JOHN WAYNE COMUNALE

For Emily, Lindsay, and my BooTour family, for Mia & Satan and their
spankable little bottoms, for Katy and Lebowski who help keep the gun out of
my mouth.

Other Titles by John Wayne Comunale

The Porn Star Retirement Plan

Charge Land

Aunt Poster

B uses. Do you realize how many people are killed by buses every day in this city? I'll save you some time by telling you that you don't. Sure, you hear about that one poor fellow every year or so who got clipped by a bus that punched his ticket, but there's always a spin on the story, like he was homeless, had no family, or he had stage four cancer or something like that.

Of course none of what we in the public hear is the truth. They don't want you to know the truth, and the *they* I am currently referring to is the Department of Public Transportation. They think if you actually knew how many people were killed by buses you would lose all faith in the system, and it would crumble. All those greedy, pencil pushing bureaucrats would be out of a job, and there was no way they could abide that, so they suppressed the truth. That truth being that there are people killed by buses not monthly, not weekly, but daily, and I know that to be true. I'm responsible for the majority of them.

Well, at least I have been for a few months now. Seven months, three weeks, four days, and ten hours to be exact. That was when I started killing daily. I mean, that was when I *had* to start killing daily if I wanted him to keep up his end of the bargain. By *him* I mean Bazael but I call him Baz for short. Baz is the . . . entity I kill for every day. Most people would mistakenly refer to him as a demon, but they just don't know there are no such things as demons.

Our relationship didn't start out like that though; with killing, I mean. At first it was a simple transaction that brought us together. An exchanging of services for an agreed upon fee, and that would be that. Except *that* wasn't that when the carrot was dangled over my head in the form of everything I ever wanted, or could hope to want. Can you blame me?

It all started innocently enough, I mean, if you can call summoning an entirely evil entity from the void to do your bidding innocent. I just needed a promotion so bad, but more so, I needed the money that came along with it. The position, the title, and the extra work could go fuck themselves, but the money, well ... I needed the money. I guess *need* is subjective in this sense because the money I was making was enough for me to live on semi comfortably. By that I mean I could pay my rent, buy the basic food-stuffs I needed to live, and occasionally have a small excess with which to grab a few beers with the boys, or treat myself to a movie every once in a while.

That was it though. There were no frills to my life because I couldn't afford them, and that included the means to entertain a young lady for the evening. If I wanted to afford a halfway decent date night I would need to pinch every penny and skip a few meals for weeks just to save enough. Even then, the money I saved wasn't enough to go on the kind of date that would impress anyone. I mostly had to settle for scraping together enough for a quickie at the 'massage parlor' a few blocks from my apartment, which was all well and good but it was starting to get boring. I had recently transitioned to masturbating alone in my apartment because it was way cheaper.

Until I met Elizabeth.

Elizabeth had long chestnut hair halting just below the outward curve of her ass, sparkling like tiny diamonds had been intricately woven throughout each strand. Her pale blue doe eyes were slightly too big for her face, which enhanced the adorableness of the rest of her features. By that I mean her small upturned nose and full but not too plump lips. She wasn't thin like a model, but maintained a frame suggesting she kept herself in shape, but it wasn't something she obsessed over. This girl, who I barely knew, became the sole motivation for the money I believed I so desperately needed.

Hence, the reason I let Baz into my life. I knew it was a long shot going in, but I wasn't in the position to rule anything out. My interest was piqued when I wandered into a magic store that had recently opened in the mall during my daily lunch hour slash daydream walk. The place was called Rabbit in the Hat, which while on the nose, was also borderline copyright infringement. I thought it was pretty weird for a magic shop to actually be opening in the mall in this present day seeing as how lame magic was, but still here it was and, with fifty minutes left of my break, I wandered in.

The place was empty, as you would expect a magic shop in a mall in the middle of the day to be. The sole occupant aside from myself was a clerk leaning back against the counter with his arms crossed and a smirk like he was the Fonz of this magic shop domain. He had semi-long, dark, wavy hair and wore a black, long sleeve button up shirt with no collar. It was tucked in to black, baggy slacks that ballooned out just below his knee where they met the top of a pair of high, black, military-style boots. His obnoxious smile was cartoonish and unnerving. It made me wonder what kind of terrible choices in life you have to make to become a clerk at a magic shop.

"Well hello there, sir, and good day to you," said the clerk, adding a half-hearted two-finger salute. "How can I meet your magic and magic-related needs today?"

"Oh, no thanks," I said, slipping my hands in my pockets and taking a look around the shop. "I just wanted to come in and see if this place was actually real, or just some joke. I thought maybe it could've been a set for a movie or something, but no, turns out this is an actual store. What the hell is a magic-related need anyway?"

It was right about then I noticed something about the clerk's outfit I had overlooked earlier. On the left side of his shirt just above his chest was a small, round pendant of a pentagram.

"What's that supposed to mean?" I asked, pointing at the pendant. "Are you able to do devil magic or something?"

"Why absolutely, sir," answered the odd looking clerk. "That happens to be our specialty."

He went on and on about how he'd made tons of deals with the devil and other demons for all kinds of stupid shit he wanted, all of it paling in comparison to the one thing I thought I needed. When

I inquired further as to how to go about said *deal making* he directed me to a number of books for sale on a shelf in the back of the store. All of a sudden I realized how stupid I was. Why was I wasting my time talking to this creepy weirdo who just wants to sell me overpriced books when I could learn everything I wanted to know about it on the Internet?

I told the clerk thanks, but no thanks, and that I'd see him on the dark side of the dungeon, and went back to work. Instead of doing any actual work I spent the rest of the day online studying up on summoning a low level demon to help me out.

It didn't turn out to be as hard as I thought it would be, the whole summoning thing, I mean. It was a little creepy and kind of smelly but not hard. The one commonality between all of the various summoning rituals was blood. Every last one of them required blood be involved in one way or another, and I do mean every single one. Some of the instructions were more specific than others as far as what type of blood and how you were to insert it into the ceremony. Some of them required goat blood, chicken blood, the blood of a one-eyed black rat and, of course, human blood—virgin or otherwise, depending.

After some quick research into butcher shops in my area I found one where I could procure pints of animal blood. The only type of blood this particular butcher had was pig and cow, so I ordered up a pint of each. The man behind the counter had a permanent sneer affixed to his face, making it hard to tell if he was suspicious of me or was passing judgment. He handed me the blood in two Styrofoam cups with the lids snapped on half-assed, allowing the crimson contents to slosh over the brim and run down the sides. He put the cups in a brown paper bag and barked a total at me, which I gladly paid before slinking out to the sidewalk to escape the butcher's glare of general disdain.

I hurried the six blocks back to my apartment and received several odd looks from the few people I passed on the street. Did they somehow know what I was up to? Had I already taken on an aura that showed people I was about to engage in nefarious occult dealings? When I arrived at the door to my building I discovered what had drawn their attention to me. The bottom of the paper bag was soaked in deep-red gore from the spillage due to the unsecured lids. I looked behind me to see I had left a Jackson Pollock-style spatter trail of blood behind as if I were using it to mark my path like a young boy in a German fairy tale. I was sure the people I passed thought I was fleeing a murder scene with my victim's heart in the bag so I could eat it later and gain their 'essence', but I couldn't do anything about it now.

I snagged a section of newspaper from in front of my neighbor's door and held it to the bottom of the bag so it wouldn't leave a bloody trail to my front door. Once inside I tossed the paper and the bag in the trash and placed the bloody Styrofoam in the sink. As I watched the spilled blood begin to make its way toward the drain I realized something. The butcher never told me which cup was which, and they weren't marked. Did he assume I would be able to tell based on appearance alone? Did he think I had such a refined palate I could merely swish a sip of the stuff around in my mouth and know beyond the shadow of a doubt which animal it came from? I'd have to remember to be more specific next time . . . if there was a next time.

I walked over to the corner of the living room I'd designated for performing the ritual. I had everything set up exactly like all the pictures I'd pulled from various Wikipedia pages on summoning ceremonies. I had the black and red candles arranged perfectly around the pentagram I'd drawn in chalk on the hardwood floor. The pages suggested I get candles made and blessed by a high-ranking witch from my local coven, but I didn't have time for that whole headache, so I just got them from Bed Bath & Beyond. A candle was a candle so I figured they'd do the trick and, besides, they were on sale. I'd gotten two squirrel skulls and one rabbit skull from a taxidermist place uptown and placed them in the appropriate spaces of the pentagram as they were depicted in my research. I couldn't tell from the pictures exactly what animal skulls they were using, and there was no specific mention in the literature, so I hoped my woodland creature combo would work.

The ritual also called for various stones and crystals to be placed at the points of the pentagram just on the inside of each candle. All I had was a geode I'd gotten from the gift shop at the science museum, three pieces of pyrite I used with my pirate costume a few Halloweens ago, and a translucent red twenty-sided die. I looked from the picture, to my setup, and back to the picture. It wasn't an exact carbon copy, but I thought it looked good enough. Besides, it's not like I needed to summon the all-powerful Dark Lord himself; I just needed any old low-level demon to poke his head out from the void, or wherever, and make it so I got the promotion. That's it. Nothing more, nothing less.

The only thing missing from my mostly accurate recreation was blood. Resting on the arm of the couch was a stack of paper stapled at the corner, and I snatched it up and began flipping through the wrinkled pages for reference. According to several of the Wiki-posts I was to put the blood into a small brass bowl and place said bowl in the center of what was, in my humble opinion, an exquisitely drawn pentagram.

I tossed the papers back over onto the couch and went back to the kitchen. I opened the cabinet to the left of the sink where I kept my bowls, but of course I didn't have anything even remotely close to the small, ornate brass ones from the pictures. The closest thing I had was a beat up, old, burnt orange Tupperware cereal bowl I had taken from my mom's house when I moved out years ago. She used to sell Tupperware back before I was born and, although she had an abundance of every type you could imagine, she only let me take the one bowl. My mom was kind of selfish like that and had major issues sharing. So much so that she never even breast-fed me as a baby because the idea of sharing her bodily fluids with her own child seemed appalling to her.

I put the bowl on the counter and it teetered on an uneven base that had been melted and warped from years of being run through the wrong cycle in the dishwasher. I took the lids off both of the blood-filled cups, picked one up in each hand, and brought them to my nose one at a time as if I were taking in the bouquet of a fine wine. They both smelled like rust and pennies mixed with wet dog, and I shrugged as I poured the contents of both into the bowl. The blood sloshed over the side, leaving telltale beads of the shiny red stuff on the cheap Formica countertop.

I walked the blood bowl over to the pentagram, being careful not to spill any more on my way. I placed it in the center just like in the picture and took a step back to admire my completed creation. Doubt began to creep in as my confidence in my shrine diminished. Taking it all in like this made me realize I had changed virtually everything from the pictures and articles I had spent precious seconds scanning over. I fished a lighter from my pocket and bent down to light the candles one at a time.

"Here goes nothing," I said aloud to no one as I switched off the table lamp to my right.

The only light in my apartment now came from the burning wicks of the five candles placed at the points of the chalk-drawn pentagram. The tiny flickers distracted me for a moment, causing me to forget what my next step was. I shook myself back into reality, snatched the papers from the couch, and flipped through them at a maddening pace until I found what I was looking for. The words. I had to say some kind of ancient incantation in a weird, creepy-sounding foreign language before completing the final step. Everything I read told me I needed to place a sacrifice in the form of 'a part of myself' into the blood bowl as the final piece to my demon-conjuring puzzle.

The examples used in my research were a bit too extreme for me. Some called for the tip of your left pointer finger, one of your toes, an eyelid, and one extreme case involved castration and the sacrificing of your man meat. I don't know how desperate you have to be to take it that far, but I bet I can guess the first thing those guys ask their demon for when he arrives. I pulled a plastic baggie containing my fingernail clippings from the last two weeks. Although fingernails weren't specifically mentioned as an option I figured, like the other substitutions I'd made, they were good enough.

I leaned over and emptied the contents of the baggie into the thirty-plus-year-old Tupperware bowl filled to the brim with a mixture of pig and cow blood. They landed softly, remaining only a moment before breaking the deep red surface tension and sinking to the bottom, making ripples so subtle they were hardly perceptible. It reminded me of watching snowflakes land just before they disappeared into the frozen moisture of the sidewalk. With the final element now in place I flipped back through the pages again until I found the words I was supposed to say to get the whole process started. I took another look at my half-assed attempt at recreating the environment needed to summon an evil being to do my bidding and shrugged.

"Here goes nothing," I said, clearing my throat to recite the incantation. "Out from the darkness, out from your realm where evil seethes. I bind you, and pull you to me to fulfill my selfish needs. Bangala, Orizam, Mecustta, Elvania, Toturus, Invitous, Leftica,

Amona!"

I realized I had raised my arms as I said the words like I was some kind of old warlock presiding over a bubbling cauldron who summoned demons all the time. I felt like an idiot, despite being by myself, and put my arms back down to my sides. Then, I watched. My eyes darted around the odd scene on the floor, searching for any signs that it was working. The candlelight flickered and danced, but that was due to my ceiling fan and not any kind of evil presence. I looked back to the stapled pages in my hand and flipped through them to make sure I hadn't forgotten some mundane detail. I went over the words again, confirming I had indeed said them all, pronouncing them to the best of my ability.

"Well fuck," I said, throwing my hands up in disgust. "Of course it wouldn't work. Why would it?"

I flung the pages over my head and kicked the twenty-sided die, sending it flying into the center of the pentagram. It smacked into the side of the blood bowl, causing the crimson contents to slosh and spill onto the chalk lines of the pentagram. The die spun off to the side, and the redirected momentum sent it under my couch. I sighed, defeated, and turned around to retrieve a towel from the kitchen to clean up my debacle of a summoning. That's when I heard it. It was like water rushing through pipes behind the thin sheetrock walls, only this sound wasn't coming from the walls. Normally I wouldn't pay much attention, dismissing the sound as the usual apartment building noises.

I turned back around slowly and searched the scene on the floor again for signs of movement. At first I saw nothing. I could still hear the whoosh of water through pipes, but now it was getting closer. Through the reflection of candlelight dancing across the surface of the blood I finally saw something. Tiny, almost imperceptible ripples were working their way out from the center of the blood bowl. While soft and subtle at first they soon grew strong enough to send blood pouring over the rim and out across the pentagram. The thick liquid smeared and blurred the piss-poor sidewalk-chalk-drawn lines making the whole thing look like a deformed spiral.

The temperature around me dropped sharply, and the hairs on the back of my neck stood up with such intensity I thought they would rip themselves from the follicles and rocket off to space. I couldn't believe it; it was working. I mean, I hoped it was working, but at this point something was at least happening and I took that to be positive.

The ripples in the bowl grew to a full-blown boil, sending even more blood across the floor and getting enough distance to extinguish one of the candles. The bowl began to shake violently with the rising intensity of the boil and leapt repeatedly from the floor. Then the boiling stopped and the bowl rested silently. I took a step forward and leaned over to get a better look at the remaining blood in the bowl. The surface was still. I took a quick look around the room, craning my neck so as to still be able to keep an eye on the bowl. Nothing seemed out of the ordinary, and there didn't appear to be any demons lurking in the shadows.

"Hello?" I called out, terrified I would actually get a response.

Nothing. Then, a beat later, a single bubble formed in the center of what blood was still in the bowl, but it didn't burst right away like the ones previous. It grew. The bubble pushed its way out across the surface until it covered the bowl like the futuristic Tupperware lid it was always meant to have. The bubble's growth halted and wobbled under its own size before finally relenting to its fragility and popping. The ceremony worked all right because now, sitting in the bowl, was what could be nothing other than an otherworldly creature.

The thing was short and squat, mimicking the girth of the blood bubble that had occupied the same space a second earlier. It was the same color as the inside of a Christmas ham before going into the oven. The pinkish, hairless skin was slick and wet with blood and what appeared to be a layer of milky-white mucus. The thing's face was scrunched up in the center of its slimy head, the top of which was adorned with tiny horns the same color as its flesh. They looked like the freshly sprouted first sprigs of green pushing their way through the dead and brown winter landscape to signify the coming spring.

Jutting from the being's back was a pair of small, featherless wings like those of a baby chick fresh from the egg. They struggled to flap against the blood and mystery goo covering them. The creature had short, stubby, human-like arms with tiny fists clenched tightly into balls. The grimace on its face communicated he was either in pain or battling a stubborn bowel movement. The stricken look suddenly melted away as the creature appeared to relax and open its eyes. They were much bigger than I thought and together the bulbous orbs filled the entire upper portion of his face. The oversized, googly-eyes were completely black without a hint of difference between pupil and iris. They were black, reflective globes staring up at me while I was staring down at them. I was still trying to wrap my head around what I was looking at when the thing suddenly spoke.

"Jesus, what a trip," it said, standing on legs just as short and stubby as its arms. "What's a guy gotta do to get a smoke around here?"

The being stepped out of the bowl, and I saw his bottom half was just as round, giving him the look of a slimy, somewhat warped bowling ball with interchangeable, satanic Mr. Potato Head-style features. He left petite, non-threatening, bloody footprints through the pentagram as he walked toward me.

"H-H-Holy shit!" I stammered. "Holllleeeeee shit!"

"Yeah, yeah. Holy shit. I get it, I get it," said the thing in the gravelly voice of a lifetime, marathon chain-smoker who had also worked in a coal mine for forty-seven years. "You know, I don't get why you're so surprised, you know that?"

"You're a . . . You're a . . . a demo—"

"Whoa, whoa, whoa there," said the thing, cutting me off. "Let's not use labels here. Just refer to me as an *embodiment of evil*. It has a much nicer ring to it."

"Okay, okay," I said, stalling in order to regain my composure. He was right; why was I surprised? I called for this . . . thing or whatever to come to me, and it did. Now it was time to get down to business. "So, now that you're here because of . . . me, doesn't that mean you have to do my bidding or something like that?"

"Relax, slick, we'll get to that in a second. Believe me, I'm as anxious as you." The short, round creature leaned forward and winked before continuing. "But first, can I get that smoke I asked for, or what?"

"Yeah, sure, of course," I babbled, sounding way more eager than I wanted to come off in my delivery. I pulled the hard pack from my back pocket and shook a single cigarette out into my palm. "Here ya go . . . buddy."

I held the cigarette out and slowly lowered it toward the creature, not sure if he would take it from me with his useless looking stubby arms or if he expected me to put it between his thin, snarled lips for him. Fortunately, the decision was made when the thing jumped up and snatched the cigarette from my shaky fingers. I worked my hand back into my pocket for a lighter, but the creature lit it himself off the flame of the closest candle. He inhaled deeply, and the smoldering red cherry tore more than halfway down the white cylinder, leaving a tremendous and impressive length of 'granny ash'.

"Ahh, that's the stuff." The beast exhaled a cloud of smoke over four times as big as his own body. "That inter-dimensional realm displacement travel always plays hell on my nerves, you know what I'm sayin'?"

"Yup," I said, placing a cigarette between my lips and lighting it in one over-practiced, fluid movement. As a rule, I didn't smoke inside but decided to make an exception based on present circumstances.

"Okay, kid," he said after another, not so lengthy puff, "let's get down to business. First of all, my name is Bazael, at your service, but just call me Baz."

"Hello, Baz. I'm . . ."

"Shut up, I don't care," spat Baz, cutting me off. His tone was more matter of fact than venomous. There was an element of professionalism to it that I found endearing. "Now, as I was saying, you're partially correct. I am here to do your bidding, however, the degree to which I can perform said *bidding* is based on what exactly you have to offer me."

"What does that mean?"

"It means based on this little . . . whatever it is you've put together here," he said, gesturing to my makeshift alter now smeared with blood to the point of being unrecognizable. "Well let's just say, this ain't gonna get you too far."

"I see," I said, taking a small drag of my cigarette. "So, what are we talking then? You know, based on . . . this."

"To be honest," he said, re-lighting one of the extinguished candles with his fingertip, "not much. The best I can do on the hexing or cursing side of things would be maybe a small pimple on the back of the neck. I could make it an ingrown hair if my aim's good enough."

"Wait, what? I don't want to give anyone a . . . pimple."

"Well, that's good actually. Because, to be honest, now that I'm looking around here, I don't think we'd be able to make a pimple happen. Don't even think about the ingrown hair either."

"Fine. Good, that's good," I spouted in my dreaded, unsuppressible eagerness. "I don't want to give anything to anyone. I want something for myself. I need something."

"Well?" asked Baz, tossing the final smoldering remains of his cigarette over his shoulder. It landed with an extinguishing hiss in the blood bowl. "Out with it already!"

"I want a promotion. I mean, I *need* a promotion so I can make enough money to be able to take this girl out and impress her enough so that she'll sleep with me."

It sounded very logical and succinct when I laid it out loud like that, and I impressed myself with the eloquence of my own proposal.

"Slow down there, chief," said Baz, holding up his stubby arms to halt my momentum. "If I just told you your offering wasn't enough to give someone a pimple, why would you think I'd be able to do all that for you?"

"Well, I . . ." I stopped short to consider the details of my request before continuing. "All I'm asking for is the promotion. I can take care of all that other stuff on my own."

"Let me break it down for you," said Baz, walking past me toward the counter that divided the living room from the kitchen. He leapt straight up to the countertop, which was surprising given the size of his legs. "But first, let me get another one of those cigarettes."

I handed the lumpy, round embodiment of evil another smoke, which he lit himself by touching it to the tip of his finger. Baz took another powerfully long puff before he continued, exhaling as he spoke.

"This entire . . . system, if you will, is based on offering and sacrifice. The bigger the request you have of me, the bigger the offering or sacrifice I need from you. Understand?"

"I think so," I said, feeling like I was being roped into the early stages of a pyramid scheme.

"While what you've done here so far—what with the fingernails and store-bought blood—may have been enough to get me here, it ain't getting you much further than that."

"Okay, I get it," I said, smashing my cigarette out on the countertop next to Baz. "Let's just cut to the chase. What's it gonna take to get me that promotion?"

"There are two ways we can go about this," said Baz, finishing his cigarette and grinding it into the counter next to mine. "First, you know your co-worker, Jim, right?"

"Sure," I replied. Jim worked in the cubicle next to mine and was a pretty solid guy. He was a lot more down to earth than most people in the office.

"Good. Then you probably know that he's your biggest competition for the promotion. So, here's your first option: you have to kill Jim, and offer him to me. That will guarantee you the job."

"Kill him? I can't kill him! I had to *buy* blood from a butcher just to perform this ceremony, and I almost backed out of that. How do you expect me to kill my co-worker?"

"It doesn't matter to me how you kill him," he said, finishing off another cigarette. "I couldn't give a shit less, to tell you the truth, but kill him you must if you want me to get you what you brought me here for."

I suddenly realized how ridiculous the situation was as I stared at the twin reflections of myself in the black, shiny eyes of Baz. It was too late now, though. Ridiculous or not, I was in too deep.

"Okay," I said, breaking eye contact with the creature so I didn't have to watch myself say this: "*Suppose* I did . . . kill Jim. Then what? Do I have to do it here in my apartment on my piece of shit, half-assed alter? How am I supposed to do that? How would I get rid of the body? How can I—"

"Whoa, whoa, whoa, slow down," interrupted Baz. "This isn't the dark ages. We've advanced in the way we, how shall I put it, handle business transactions. You don't have to bring him here, you just have to be wearing this when you off him."

Baz's eyes, nose, and mouth migrated to the top of his head, and I realized he had turned to look directly at the ceiling. His rubbery, round body's movements weren't easily discernable due mostly to its shape. Baz opened his mouth wide enough to split himself down the middle and somehow managed to reach down his own throat using his impossibly stubby arm. His arm stretched like a pre-CGI, claymation, practical effect until it landed on what it was searching for. Baz began making a horridly grotesque choking sound as his arm appeared to switch gears. His gags were like the barks of a sea lion just as a great white bit through its windpipe. Then the gagging stopped and the process started over in reverse. When the arm emerged from the cavity of the beast, his fist was gripped tight around a dirty gold chain with a medallion dangling from it. Both the chain and medallion were covered in thick, slimy phlegm that dripped in slow motion due to its sheer density.

Baz closed his mouth, returning it to its original size, and the rest of his features returned to the front of his head. He shook the sludge from the object he'd retrieved and thrust it out for me to take. With the majority of the mystery fluid removed I could now see what it was, or at least what I thought it was.

"Is that a . . . a . . ." I stammered, pointing at the medallion hanging from the chain.

"Yes, it's a small nugget of shit made from pure gold," snapped Baz.

"Wow, really? Because that *is* what it looks like, but there was no way I thought that's what it really was. You know? I guess I just thought it was going to be a pentagram or something?"

"Most people do but it's not, okay! It's a golden shit nugget because it always has been, and it always will be, and that's that!"

"Okay, okay," I said, backing off. "I'm sorry I even said anything."

"Here, take it," said Baz, shoving the chain at me again. "All you have to do is wear it when you kill the guy, and you'll get the credit for the sacrifice. You have to be wearing the gold shit nugget when you do it though, or it doesn't count. There are no exceptions. Understand?"

I took the chain, grasping it gingerly between my thumb and forefinger, holding it away from my body as I would a poisonous snake. I brought it closer slowly and got a good look at the thing. It was surprisingly detailed and lifelike from the porous texture of the outer layer to the piece of half-chewed corn pushing partially out from the bumpy underside. For a literal gold hunk of shit it was quite beautiful in an off-putting way.

"I have one question," I said.

"Yeah, what?"

"Do I have to be wearing it where it can be seen, or can I hide it under my shirt? Or even under two or three shirts?"

"Jesus Christ," moaned Baz. "Yes, it can be covered up, you just have to be wearing it. That's it."

"That's it, huh?"

And that's how it started; innocently and with regret, as most strange new things do before they get easy. The day I killed Jim I hadn't even planned on doing it. I was still trying to figure out a game plan and work up the courage. The otherworldly being of evil had been living with me at my apartment for the last week, waiting on me to pull the trigger. The novelty of Baz was starting to wear off, as all he did was chain-smoke and watch TV all day, waiting for me to shit or get off the pot. It was time for me to shit.

Like I said, I wasn't planning on killing anyone that day, but everything just happened to fall into place. I was about twenty yards from the stop where Jim caught the bus every morning, leaning up against the wall of a convenience store. I was wearing my ratty old Mets cap and dark sunglasses, trying to look inconspicuous, but I knew Jim couldn't see me from where he stood anyway. I was wearing the golden turd around my neck, as I had been from the time Baz gave it to me.

It wasn't my idea, but he told me I should keep it on just in case the opportunity to kill Jim presented itself to me. He said that way I'd always be prepared and wouldn't have to run to my car or apartment to retrieve it since, by then, I'd most likely have lost my nerve. He wasn't wrong, and as I lightly fingered the bit of corn on the underside of the poop nugget I was struck by inspiration. Maybe the sacred and evil object had something to do with it, or maybe I'd finally come to terms with what I had to do, but either way I was about to do it. I stepped out of the shadows of the convenience store and called out.

"Hey Jim!" I yelled, removing my sunglasses so he would recognize me.

He took a second to respond, staring me down, but he finally managed a confused half-wave.

"Hey, come down here for a second," I said, stepping closer to the curb, waving for him to come to me.

Jim looked perplexed, pointed at his watch, then up at the bus stop sign. I knew he was trying to pantomime that the bus would be there any second, but that's exactly what I was counting on.

"Look, I know but this is really important!" I hollered up the sidewalk, refusing to take a step toward him.

"I don't want to be late for work!" he yelled back, giving up the miming.

"I know, but this *is* about work. It'll only take a second!"

Jim looked at his watch again, threw up his hands, and began walking to me. He was clearly agitated as he approached, but I held my ground and waited. I was in the optimal position for what I needed to do.

"Well?" asked Jim, shrugging begrudgingly. "What's this all about? What's so important that I had to walk down here to you? You know my bus is about to be here."

From behind me I heard the grinding whir of the old city bus turning the corner and heading down the street toward us.

"See, there's the bus now," said Jim, pointing emphatically over my shoulder at the silver tube lumbering up the street. "I have to go."

He turned to head back to the stop, but I grabbed his arm and held him in place. He tried to pull away, but my grip held tight.

"What are you doing? Are you insane? Let go of me!" Jim's tone went from angry to frightened in a matter of ten syllables.

"Just wait one more second," I said calmly, still holding tight. "I told you this is important."

Jim started to say something back to me, but my focus was on the sound of the approaching bus. I could picture it getting closer and closer as its massive diesel engine propelled the behemoth. I tuned back in to Jim's voice at the last second.

"Let go you idiot, I'm going to miss the—"

Before he finished his sentence I pivoted and used the entirety of my body weight to fling him into the street. His toes just scraped the pavement as the grime-covered grill of the bus delivered the hard kiss of death to his face. His skull buckled against the impact and caved in like a soft melon rind dropped on the floor of a filthy produce department. Orange and red jelly burst from the holes in his face and head like a thick, wet fireworks finale on the Fourth of July. The momentum propelled him back only an inch before his feet were sucked up under the bumper and he was slammed down to the street. His body crunched under the front set of tires before the bus driver could even begin to apply the brakes.

That was all I saw. I turned from the street, put my sunglasses back on, and started walking in the opposite direction. I heard the screams, but blocked everything out as I put my head down and walked. I was a block away before I realized I was clutching the golden turd medallion in my left hand. I couldn't tell if it was warm because I was holding it so tightly, or for some other reason. I thought I heard Baz laughing somewhere far off in my head, but I knew I had to be imagining it. I kept expecting to be tackled from behind by some brave citizen who'd witnessed my dastardly deed, but it never happened. No one even called after me. I snuck a glimpse back up the sidewalk as I rounded the corner and could clearly see no one was looking in my direction.

My confidence swelled with each step I took until I thought my chest would burst. I'd never felt any emotion that intensely in my entire life, and it made me wonder if I'd been missing out on something. I was not prepared for the lack of regret I felt over what I'd just done. It was easy. It was empowering. I liked it. I liked it a lot. I was so inside my head I didn't hear the ambulance screaming up the street until it raced past me, and even then I was hardly aware. I was riding a high I wanted to make last the rest of the walk home, and last it did until the moment I opened the door to my apartment.

"Well, it's about time. I thought I was going to have to start having my mail forwarded to this dump."

Baz's voice came out of the darkness, and I flipped on the light to find him standing on the counter. An expression I could only best approximate as a smile was smeared across the facial area of the formless being.

"Yeah," I said dazedly as the weight of what I'd done finally started to push down on my insides like a trash compactor crushing my soul. "Yeah, I . . . I guess I finally did it."

"Damn right you did," said Baz, plucking a cigarette from the air around his head. He'd been doing that for a while, citing that my cigarettes weren't strong enough for him so he needed some from his own realm. "And you know what that means?"

"I think it means that I'm a murderer."

"What? No," said Baz, blowing smoke at me as I locked the door and threw my keys on the counter next to him. "Well, technically I guess it does, but that's not the point. The point is now you can have what you wanted. The only competition you had for the promotion you want is dead, meaning you're a shoo-in, and I got my sacrifice which guarantees you're a shoo-in because I've already taken care of it."

The feeling of my soul being slowly compacted faded into the back of my mind when Baz said this, and I actually felt excitement creep in to put an obscuring smear across my doubts.

"Taken care of? What do you mean by 'taken care of?'" I put my palms down flat on the counter and leaned in closer to Baz.

"Just what I said," he replied, pulling another of his special cigarettes from the ether and lighting it with the dying cherry of the one he was currently smoking. "They haven't heard the unfortunate news about Jim back at your office yet, but they've already made the decision to give the promotion to you."

"Really?"

"Yes, really. They're telling you tomorrow when you come in."

I'd taken the day off today, citing an appointment for my yearly physical, so no one was expecting me in the office. I flashed to a scene of me getting to work tomorrow and having to pretend I had no idea about Jim as mourning co-workers stopped me in the parking garage to deliver the bad news. I would act surprised, shocked, and devastated at the same time, all the while knowing about the good news I would be handed shortly after getting in the building. All of a sudden a dark wave of anxiety crashed against me, drenching me in paranoia. Could I really trust this chain-smoking, magical monster?

"Are you sure it worked though? I mean, I don't want to show up tomorrow and find out they've eliminated the position, or are putting off the announcement due to Jim's death, or something like that."

"Fine," said Baz, exhaling smoke as he spoke.

He rolled his eyes, snapped his fingers, and my phone started ringing. I plunged my hand into my pocket to retrieve it and saw it was a call from the office's main secretary, Nancy. She was always nice to me but was, without a doubt, the most catty person in the office, and she loved to gossip. I put the phone to my ear and said hello.

"Hey, sugar, it's Nancy," she said in her soft southern accent. "I know you're at the doctor's office, but I just had to call you. Am I interrupting?"

"Uh, no," I stammered into the phone. "Not at all, I'm just sitting in the waiting room."

"Well, you are not going to believe this but you know Jim? He was hit by a bus this morning and killed. Can you believe it?"

"What? Oh my . . . that's . . . that's terrible. I . . . I don't know what to say . . ."

I hoped my act sounded sincere over the phone since I hadn't had time to practice.

"I know," she continued, "it's just awful, but I have something else to tell you too."

"What's that?"

"Well, Dean and the other higher-ups sent paperwork to me earlier this morning to update your information with payroll and HR."

"My information?"

"Yeah, sugar, you got that promotion! Oh, be sure to act surprised when they tell you tomorrow. Gotta go now."

The phone went dead, and I slowly pulled it away from my ear. Baz stood with what was an unmistakable smirk on his face, and his short, fat arms crossed confidently below his chin. His eyes screamed *I told you so* up at me as he nodded slowly.

"Now that you know I'm not full of shit," he said, "allow me to make another proposal to you."

I don't like to think Baz had any influence over me or my actions because I typically pride myself on my freethinking, obstinate attitude of doing exactly what I want all the time. Now I'm so deep into this give-and-take relationship we have I'm not sure who's calling the shots anymore. I try not to think about what my life would be like if I'd just stopped and not let that smooth-talking demon convince me otherwise.

He was good at it though. Really good.

The day I killed Jim and came home to find my wish had been granted I was overwhelmed with a swirl of contradicting thoughts and feelings all battling to resonate with validity upon my conscience. Baz got results though, that was for sure, and it was quite hard to find fault in his logic. He told me I could go on with my new promotion and hope the rest of my plan fell into place, but there was no guarantee. Just because I would now have the funds available to take Elizabeth out on a proper date didn't mean she would actually *want* to go out with me. She was always pleasant at the office, but what if she was just being . . . friendly? In fact, Baz reminded me that with a new position came more responsibility and more work, which meant I might not even have time to take her on a date, let alone attempt to start any semblance of a relationship.

Baz had only been at my place for a week and he already knew how to manipulate me like he'd known me for years. Manipulation was clearly a skill he'd mastered long ago. I was crestfallen at the thought of the promotion blowing up in my face.

"Listen," Baz said to me, lighting yet another cigarette, "it was easy, wasn't it? You might as well do it again? I mean, it just makes sense at this point."

The lights dimmed around him as he spoke, and my head swirled with the weight of what I'd just done, but perhaps even worse, I saw just how easy it would be to do again. Baz had made me sing for my supper, and now he wanted the encore we both knew I was aching to give. He was making perfect sense. I'd already gone to the trouble, albeit slightly half-assed, of actually summoning this creature from the void, or wherever, so I might as well ride this thing out and milk it for all I could.

"So if I really want my . . . let's just call it my *plan* to work out," I slowed myself down, thinking about each word carefully before I chose it, "I would really have to kill someone else?"

"Basically, yes," spat Baz.

"Are there requests that don't require killing, or can you bank some points from one to use on something else?"

"Afraid not. Think of it as a balancing out of . . . things."

"What things?"

"Energy actually," he continued. "There are different energies around us at all times that wax and wane constantly to maintain this balance. Your kind usually can't differentiate between them except for in certain rare cases. There is a type of energy I manipulate to make the things you want happen, and that energy has to be replaced or the whole of existence across all planes would be thrown off balance."

"Won't the energy just be replaced, or 'balanced', or whatever like you said anyway?"

"Sure, when it happens organically it all takes care of itself. When an ugly, little fuck like me is reaching across planes to manipulate said energy, and effectively snatch it away . . . Well, that ain't exactly organic."

"Is that true? It sounds like bullshit."

"Bullshit?" Baz recoiled with incredulity at my question. "Yeah sure, I'm making this all up, because I didn't just get you a promotion when you did what I told you to. Oh wait, yes I did. I'm putting it in the simplest terms for you since, being a human, there's no way you can wrap your brain around the concept of balancing out existence."

"Why do you want to do this for me so bad? What do you get out of it?"

"Let's just say it boosts my street cred back home, and leave it at that. Besides, I like hanging out in your apartment way better than the shithole I live in."

"Okay, okay," I said, throwing my hands up, "let's just say I do believe you. Why does each . . . *thing* you do for me essentially cost a human life?"

"Don't ask me," said Baz, lighting another cigarette and walking across the counter toward my random liquor bottles bunched up in the corner. "That just happens to be the type of energy it takes to replace what I use to, for lack of a better way to put it, grant your wish. All of it gets sent back and forth through the necklace, which is why you need to wear it when you do the deed. Otherwise, you'd just be killing people in cold blood for no reason."

I thought what I'd just done was cold-blooded either way, and I reached my hand up to clutch the golden poop nugget dangling from the chain around my neck. I had forgotten I was wearing it, but the reminder was enough to put me strangely at ease. I felt that confidence begin to rise in me and quickly decided I didn't care. Cold-blooded or not, I was in. If it was that easy for me to get what I wanted without having to put any work in, or worry about failing, I'd be stupid not to be. Killing Jim was pretty easy and, surprisingly, not as offensive to my moral compass as I thought it might be.

"Okay," I said, walking toward Baz scrutinizing my liquor collection. "Let's do it!"

I extended my hand and he regarded it with a devilish smile on the fat, round area that could only best be described as 'face-like'.

"Well, I admit I thought you'd spend more time thinking about it, but I am pleased with the efficient way in which you process information and weigh your options."

I wasn't sure if I'd done exactly that—the option weighing part, that is—and maybe I should have taken longer to consider all the moving pieces involved in Baz's proposal, but I don't think it would have changed my answer. I'd been working hard my entire life with nothing to show for it and chances were it would always be that way. I didn't want to work hard anymore for an almost non-existent reward but, more than that, I didn't want to work anymore at all. This was exactly what Baz was offering me, and all I had to do was push someone in front of a bus from time to time? It didn't seem like a bad deal to me at all.

Baz reached his short, fat nub of an arm out to me as far as he could, and I closed the distance between us to take his hand. We shook, and Baz pulled away to mix some drinks for us to celebrate our new alliance. He pushed a glass tumbler toward me, filled to the top with translucent gold firewater. It sloshed over the brim as I took it in my hand, and the boozy contents dripped across my knuckles. Baz quickly replicated the drink in a tumbler of his own and raised it up in a toast.

"You're making a great decision," he said. "You won't be disappointed."

We clinked glasses and chucked the liquor-heavy concoctions down our throats where it burned like a match flame chasing after a gasoline trail. The liquid converged in my stomach and exploded, sending a full-blown, raging, monster fireball back up the way it came. I stopped the heat missile with the back of my teeth and swallowed, sending the blaze below before I was able to speak again. I cleared my throat and slammed my hands down flat on the counter in front of Baz.

"Okay," I said, trying to look him in the eye, but the intoxicating effects of the strong drink were already making it hard for me to focus. "Who do I have to kill next?"

That was all it took to get me 'in the habit,' for lack of a better way to put it. Baz didn't waste any time, and we immediately set to putting a plan together for the next 'sacrifice'. According to Baz, the next sacrifice was a no brainer. If I wanted a sure-thing date with Elizabeth I was going to have to kill her husband.

"What? Wait, what? I mean really, what?!" I was floored and stammering. "Husband? I didn't know she was married!"

"Of course she's married," said Baz with casual nonchalance as he pulled another cigarette from the ether above his head. "A choice broad like that, what did you think?"

"I–I–I guess I don't know what I thought," I managed, "but I did not think she was married, that's for sure."

"And did you think the ring she wore was just a personal fashion statement?"

"Well . . . yeah, I guess. I didn't pay that much attention."

"Yeah, well, you don't have to worry about details now that you got me around," said Baz as he lit the cigarette and inhaled deeply, turning half of it to ash instantly.

"It doesn't matter if I have you," I snapped. "The deal is off! She has a husband, for Christ's sake, and I don't see how killing him is going to even give me a shot with her let alone be a 'sure thing'! The last thing she would want to do is get together with me right after her husband dies. It's done! It's over!"

I turned my back on Baz and slunk to the other end of the counter to silently sulk. How could I be so stupid to not even know she was married? Now I got this stupid promotion for nothing. I just added a ton of extra work and stress to my life, and I don't even get the girl. I wondered if it was too late to change things back to the way they were. Maybe Baz could undo my promotion, bring Jim back to life, and make it so the two of us never met? From behind me I heard Baz clear his throat to get my attention, and I slowly turned around.

"Allow me to explain," he said calmly, still smoking and swigging his drink. "Let's just say you still want me to help you with Elizabeth, but instead of her husband you kill someone else for the trade off. Sure, no big deal. I do my thing, Elizabeth falls for you, and leaves her lame-o husband in the lurch. Sounds good, right? Wrong. Now you have to deal with a jealous ex and all the drama and baggage that come along with him. He'll be completely blindsided by her leaving, and will more than likely have an adverse reaction that will most definitely affect you. However, if *he* is the sacrifice then it becomes a whole 'two birds, one stone' type of thing. You understand?"

Shit.

Baz was absolutely right. I'd already committed to the idea of killing a person in exchange for the guaranteed affection of Elizabeth, so what difference did it all of a sudden make that the person happened to be her husband? My morals were beyond corrupt at this point, and Baz did make a very good point. If Elizabeth left him out of the blue for me, who knew how he may react? He could come after me and try to kick my ass or worse. He could flip out on her and make our new life together a living hell, which would make me want him dead, which I would ask Baz to do, which meant I would have to . . .

"Dammit," I muttered under my breath.

"Excuse me?" asked Baz. "You okay, man? You kind of went away there for a second. Were you talking to me?"

"No. Nothing. I mean, yeah."

"Yeah? Yeah what?"

"Yeah, you're right. You're right, let's do it your way. I'll take care of her husband, and you . . . you just take care of your end. O-okay?"

"Glad you're seeing it my way now, kid," said Baz, smiling in his awkward way. "Trust me, you will not regret this."

I almost didn't use a bus to kill Elizabeth's husband, but not from lack of trying. I followed the guy when he left their apartment the next morning to see which bus he took to work. We had the day off again on account of Jim's brutal death at the hands of the city's Public Transportation System, so it worked out great for me. I made some notes on the area surrounding the particular bus stop including vantage points, potential approach patterns, and how many people were around at that time.

I went home and looked over my notes, trying to come up with a plan without so much as a sign of interest on Baz's part. He just sat on the sofa chain-smoking while he binge-watched *Lost*. I didn't care that he didn't want to help me because I knew how pissed he was going to be when he got to the finale, so I was okay with figuring it out on my own. It wasn't like I hadn't just done the same thing a day and a half ago, and I had improvised the whole thing then. Besides, his job was to make with the magic, and my job was to make with the sacrifice. I could handle my end on my own.

The next morning I was up before the sun and at Elizabeth's husband's bus stop hours before he would be heading there. I wanted to take in the lay of the land one more time just in case I'd missed something, and I wanted to walk through my plan. I stood there trying to visualize every nuance of what I was about to do. I was no professional. I had gotten lucky last time, but there was no guarantee lightning would strike twice. I wanted to be prepared.

I paced the two-by-five section of sidewalk in front of the bus stop bench, muttering encouragement under my breath to psych myself up. People started showing up to the stop, which halted my pacing and sent me off down the street to make the block. I had almost forty minutes before Elizabeth's husband would be there, and although I knew three different buses would come and go in that time, I didn't want to risk anyone who could potentially be there later seeing me hanging around. Being inconspicuous was not something I took into account the first time, and it weighed heavy on my mind this time around.

I turned the corner, absently fingering the gold poop nugget through my shirt where it rested against my bare chest. Something about just touching it was enough to ease my anxiety and even my temper. I figured it was just some kind of psychosomatic association-type bullshit, but I didn't care. I'd just grown accustomed to the thing, that's all. I walked into a coffee shop halfway down the street and stood at the counter, waiting to be served. Just as I was about to order a quad macchiato I saw him. Elizabeth's husband was sitting in the café drinking a cup of coffee.

He looked up in the direction of the counter and our eyes met for a brief half second before he looked back at his phone. My stomach crashed down into my crotch, then leapt up to hit me in the throat before finally settling back in place, and I realized I hadn't been nervous until this moment. I liked the idea of total anonymity, and although we hadn't officially met, the eye contact alone was enough for me. As far as I was concerned I might as well have just walked up to him, introduced myself, and told him I was going to kill him in about thirty minutes, so he should enjoy his coffee while he could.

"I said, do you want your change or what?"

The haughty voice of the barista snapped me from my trance, and I could tell from her tone she'd been trying to get my attention throughout the entirety of my daydream.

"Oh, sorry," I sputtered. "I haven't had my coffee yet. You can keep the change."

I moved down the counter to retrieve my drink and winced at

the cheesiness of my statement. I'm sure she heard that a hundred times a day, and it was just as equally not funny when I said it. I kept my head down so as not to draw any further attention to myself from my current 'mark', or anyone else. It was quite possible there were other people in the coffee shop that would be catching the same bus, so I wanted to act as inconspicuous as possible.

The last thing I needed was for someone to take notice of me here, then see me again in a few minutes hanging around their bus stop acting creepy. It would be easy for someone to get suspicious after seeing me in both places just before one of their fellow users of public transportation was run down by the bus. When asked by the police if they saw anything out of the ordinary they could say: *"Yeah actually, I saw some weirdo creeping around the coffee shop staring at people, then I saw the same guy walking quickly away from the accident. Describe him? Sure can. I even took a picture of him on my phone because he was just so . . . creepy."*

I slunk away from the counter with my coffee, keeping my head down, and slipped out the exit while trying to put these thoughts out of my head. I stepped out onto the sidewalk and headed around the block. I still had plenty of time before Elizabeth's husband would head to the stop, and I needed to clear my head. I thought about calling the whole thing off. Maybe I should just regroup and come back the next day, but then I felt the weight of the golden turd press against my chest and I started to calm down. The mysterious amulet was hidden beneath two shirts and a jacket, and I swore I felt it grow warm against my sensitive pink skin, but dismissed it as being a byproduct of all the layers I had on.

I rounded the corner heading back toward the bus stop and my confidence rose with each step until I felt invincible. A few minutes ago I was biding my time and talking myself out of the whole thing, but now I cursed the slow tick of each second. This wasn't the same feeling I had when I killed Jim. That was all confused nerves and adrenaline, but this time was different. This time I was excited. I started to think the odd amulet was responsible for imbuing me with my newfound courage.

I leaned up against the side of a closed furniture store about twenty yards from the bus stop behind a column built into the wall to keep myself hidden from the growing group waiting for the bus. It was getting close to time for Elizabeth's husband's bus, but he was nowhere to be seen. I anxiously watched the group check their watches in anticipation of their approaching mode of transportation. As I kept my eye on the stop, making sure to stay out of sight, I felt someone approaching from the opposite direction and turned just in time to see Elizabeth's husband walk past. He must have taken the long way around the block like I did, which was not what I expected. He glanced up and our eyes met once again. The moment was much briefer than at the coffee shop, but I could see the recognition in his eyes.

This threw me off more than I thought it would, and I reeled mentally from the shock and began to feel lightheaded. It was just for a moment though, because the loud grinding engine of the bus sounding from the end of the block snapped me back into a laser-like focus. I paused to pat the golden piece of shit beneath my shirts before I sprung into action. All of my planning went out the window since I had prepared for him to come from the opposite direction, but now everything was turned around. It was backwards, the bus was approaching, and I needed to adapt fast.

"Hey," I called, leaping out from the partial safety of the pillar. "Hey man, wait up. Yeah, you."

Elizabeth's husband turned halfway when he realized I was talking to him. He slowed down, looked up the street at his approaching bus, then back to me.

"Sorry," he said, not stopping. "I don't have any change and I need to catch this bus. Maybe next time, buddy."

I was taken aback for a half-second, wondering if I put out the general vibe of a panhandling bum, but quickly got back on point. The bus was coming. There was no more time for hesitation.

"No, no. I don't need money, I mean, I was just . . . Hey, aren't you Elizabeth's husband?"

This got his attention enough to slow him down and turn to face me.

"Yeah," he said with a puzzled look. He glanced back over his shoulder at the bus coming up the street before continuing. "Yeah, that's me. Do I know you?"

"Yeah, well . . . no, not really," I replied quickly, well aware of my fast closing window of opportunity. "I know Elizabeth, I mean, from work. I work with her."

"Oh yeah," he said, extending his hand. "Sorry I don't remember if we've met. My name is Jack. Liz told me about your co-worker, Jim. I was sorry to hear about that, but I really can't talk right now. My bus is here."

I had never heard Elizabeth called Liz before, and my heart warmed at the thought that it would soon be me calling her that amongst other pet names we would come up with for each other. The thought captivated me in such a way I almost didn't realize he'd turned back around to hurry toward the approaching bus.

"Oh yeah," I said jogging to catch up to him. "I'm on this bus too."

Jack slowed so I could match his stride and let his guard down just a bit, which was all I needed. The bus was stopped now and the waiting people had fallen in line to get on. The short line snaked down the side of the bus, and Jack and I took our places at the back. I had to think fast since I was less than thirty seconds away from missing my opportunity completely. I looked down to see Jack's shoelace hanging limply, dragging on the sidewalk, and was struck by inspiration.

"Where are you headed?" he asked. "I take this bus every morning and don't think I've ever seen—"

That was all he got out since I had stepped down firmly on his dangling shoelace, causing him to lose his balance as he attempted to advance in line. He stumbled at first and waved his hands around to grab at air that would not restore his balance, then he fell. Not hard, but hard enough to drop the leather messenger bag he was carrying, scattering its contents on the sidewalk. This happened just as the last person in front of us climbed onto the bus.

"Ah shit," said Jack, clearly miffed over the incident. "What the fuck, man? The bus . . ."

I was down on the sidewalk at his level in a flash, apologizing profusely, taking the blame and pretending to help him gather his papers. The bus driver hadn't noticed us, and the door closed with a pneumatic hiss. Jack scurried madly to grab his papers with one hand and beat on the side of the bus with the other to get the driver's attention. He went to stand up, but I grabbed his shirt and pulled him back down to the sidewalk as the bus began to pull away.

"What the—"

That was all Jack got out as I let go of his shirt and pushed him off the curb just in time to be crushed beneath the bus's rear tires. Our eyes met again one final time as Jack realized what was happening, just before his skull was pulverized between pavement and steel-banded, heavy-duty, black rubber. My chest burned where the poop amulet rested against it, and I put my hand to my face to cover my smile just before standing up to start screaming.

"Oh my god!" I yelled. "Help! Someone help! He's under the bus!"

In the realm of Okanisis, beyond the invisible fabric that shrouds the Old Ones and the Dark Ones from the limited perception of human beings, a black sun climbed slowly into the sky. It peaked over craggy mountain ranges equally as black and feverishly burned against a garish red the color of the hottest fire. Okanisis isn't Hell because Hell doesn't exist but, by comparison, if you were familiar with legend, myth, and folklore, Okanisis was much worse. This is, in fact, the place where all of Earth's evil comes from due to the ease with which those who dwell there can pass back and forth between the two realms. This, of course, is no accident.

The various entities, imps, and godheads that live there are bored and restless, and yearn to use the full potential of their power, which is impossible due to the confining energy of this place. Okanisis has been corrupted and devastated more times over than anyone or anything can count or remember. Now it serves mainly as a weigh station for evil to bide its time before crossing over to flex its horrible muscle, but before all that it was the Old Ones who crossed over to plant the seeds which would open doors between the two worlds for eternity.

These doors can at times be opened by power-hungry, ego-driven humans on Earth who yearn for power they were never meant to have. Power they lack the capacity to even begin to understand how to control, but it's this insatiable selfishness in humans that the Old Ones rely on. It is the catalyst that allows for the crossing over. The entities with the power to cause the most destruction take long trips into the human realm and exert their commanding will upon those who seek their help. However, even the strongest beings must come back to Okanisis because, in a place of such chaos and suffering, there is still an order to things that must be strictly followed.

Bazael is from Okanisis, but he was never supposed to leave. It wasn't his time in the grand scheme of things as kept in check by the original Old Ones of the realm. Now that he has escaped he is doing his best to make sure he never comes back to Okanisis by corrupting a human to the extent of being completely reliant upon him. Once he achieves this he will be able to fuse himself to said human and to the world he lives in. This isn't a new trick by any means and has been attempted before by many lower level beings of Okanisis. In fact it was Mephistopheles who first pulled off the trick of escaping. Hundreds of thousands of years have passed since then, and his own arrogance became his ultimate undoing, which is almost always the cause of great falls from glory. Once Mephistopheles began to allow himself to appear in the work of the writers he was corrupting it acted like a trail of breadcrumbs leading the Old Ones right to him. Since being returned to Okanisis he has not been seen and is only talked about in hushed whispers.

Mandiba has been made aware of Bazael's escape by those who keep Okanisis and its inhabitants in line and has been charged with bringing him back to restore the order. Mandiba is no stranger to this type of work as it is his specialty, being a *Seeker of the Lost*. He has hunted countless escapees throughout eons who have attempted the same type of feat, and he has brought back every single one of them without fail. Even now Mandiba could sense Baz's presence through the activities he convinced his human counterpart to carry out, but for some reason he could not hone in on exactly where he was.

There was an unknown energy interfering with his usual sharp tracking skills, and he figured Baz had stumbled onto a way to interrupt his signal and to make himself harder to find. This meant

Baz wasn't on some usual trouble-making joyride of a trip to Earth. He was trying to buy himself time. He was up to something. Mandiba wasn't worried at all by this development, as he knew it was only temporary. He would find Baz soon enough and bring him back home where he belonged.

For someone whose only transgression on society thus far has been a handful of moving violations, I felt surprisingly collected for having killed two people in two days. Everything went so smoothly I couldn't help but wait for the other shoe to drop, but so far it hadn't happened and I was starting to think it never would. I knew I was drinking my own Kool-Aid, and thinking like that was dangerous, but I just felt so damn good it was hard not to.

The image of Jack's head being crushed by the bus tires was tattooed on the inside of my eyelids, but not in a bad way. I wanted to see it. I was proud of what I'd done. I was surprised by just how easily his skull collapsed under the weight of the steel-tube behemoth with a crunch like a child stomping a pinecone on his walk to school. His eyes had grown wide with what I thought was surprise until they burst from their sockets, and I realized the effect was caused by the enormous pressure pushing down on him. It made me smile and think of the cartoons I watched insatiably as a child. Just like with Jim, no one had seen what I'd done and I, in fact, looked like a hero for calling attention to what everyone assumed was a horrible accident.

My story never wavered and stayed word for word consistent as I told it to the beat cop who showed up first, the sergeant who arrived shortly after, the detective and his partner, the 'lead' detective, and finally the investigator from public transportation in charge of accidents. I impressed myself by being able to come up with something so detailed and succinct on the fly like I did. I'd never been very good at thinking quick on my feet, but when I started talking, my words flowed smooth like I imagined the skin on the back of Liz's neck to be. The poop amulet burned with noticeable but not unpleasant warmth when I talked to each authority figure, and the warmth brought me the same calmness it had the day before.

My story went thusly:

I walked to the bus stop just as the doors opened and took my place at the back of the line. How often do I ride this bus? Every day, and it's usually on time for the most part. Anyway, the man in front of me bent down to tie his shoe, and I guess the driver didn't see us waiting because she closed the doors and started to take off. This surprised myself and the man in front of me, who was still on one knee, and we both started yelling and banging on the bus, trying to get the driver's attention. It all happened so fast, and I know I've always heard people say that about these things, but I'll tell you it's true. I didn't see how he fell exactly since I was pounding, but I guess he lost his balance getting up, because all of a sudden he was under the bus and the sound . . . well, I imagine I'll be haunted by it my entire life.

There were no other witnesses around paying enough attention to prove or disprove the truthfulness of my statement, but several of them commented on the sound. They heard the crunch, and while I was acting the part, they were truly affected by it.

Although I was stuck at the scene of the 'accident' for hours, the time raced by, and it was already mid-afternoon before I even bothered to check my watch. My being a witness and having to give several statements took a lot of time but I didn't have to work, so I wasn't worried about it. I knew my promotion was solid and would be waiting for me. The authorities called Elizabeth who, of course, rushed down to the scene.

Unfortunately, due to the amount of necessary protocol that must be followed when a city vehicle is involved in a fatal accident they couldn't move Jack's body for some time. Elizabeth was forced to take in the image of her pancake-headed late husband for several hours. Her expression appeared to grow more distant and less mournful by the minute, and I wondered if Baz's magic was already beginning to kick in. I pushed the thought away, mostly out of fear I would grow too confident and say or do something that would make me seem suspicious. I'd done my part and I was sure Baz would do his, so I had no reason to worry. Besides, even if the spell had kicked in, now was not the time or place to do anything about it.

When I was finally cleared to leave I gave Elizabeth a hug goodbye and imagined the embrace to be tighter than it actually was. I told her softly she could give me a call if she needed to talk, lingered in her eyes for just a moment, then turned and headed down the sidewalk in the direction of my building. The further I got down the street the wider my smile became, so I pulled my hat down further and buried my chin in my chest to hide the smirk. When I rounded the corner I couldn't hold it in any longer and started giggling.

At first it was a quiet titter like children trying not to be heard in the back of the classroom, but a few steps later it erupted into a full-blown, knee-slapping laughter that made my eyes water. I didn't even realize I had pulled the gold poop nugget out from beneath my shirts and was clutching it tightly in my fist until the heat it gave off was too much to ignore. I let it go and left it hanging out of my shirt to dangle from my neck in full view of anyone who cared to notice. When I arrived at my building I tucked the amulet back behind the protective double cotton layer of clothing and headed in to my apartment.

Mandiba sat cross-legged on one of the few flat surfaces available atop the ashy black mountains of Okanisis. Carved into
a small patch of rock in front of him were a series of sigils and
symbols he'd drawn into the stone with one of the talons perched
upon his fingertips like giant sharp candy corns made of polished
bone and razor wire. These symbols would be foreign to even the
most scholarly of occultists, but for Mandiba they were what allowed him to see beyond the gossamer barrier between Okanisis
and the realm where Earth existed.

The black moon, which was one of four, hung low in the sky
just above where he sat, which was no accident. He used the
unique frequencies emitted by the black moon coupled with his
knowledge of an ancient, symbol-based art form Earth dwellers
called magic to search for those he'd been charged with finding.
His eyes were closed as his mind plunged deep into the energy being fed to him, but his stern, slate-gray face was knotted with fits of
frustration. He'd climbed the deathly mountains higher than he'd
ever gone before in order to be as close to the black moon as possible so he could harness the full extent of its mysterious energy,
but for some reason it wasn't enough.

Usually when Mandiba went deep into his trances he was able

to clearly see the offending entity. He could tell exactly where they were, hone in on them, and project himself there to snatch them back to the place they were never meant to leave. Not this time though, and while it confused him, he was enraged more than anything. The only thing he was able to clearly see was the energy of Baz and that it was somewhere it didn't belong but nothing else. Everything surrounding his energy was cloaked in a thick gray fog of confusion. Usually when a problem like this came up while Mandiba was seeking he could dig until he found traces of the escapees' energy left like psychic fingerprints by the human cattle they were currently corrupting, but now he couldn't even find that.

Mandiba knew something wasn't right about this, and he dismissed a thought that jumped into his mind, but not before it had a chance to leave a brief impression. Baz wasn't working alone, but Mandiba wasn't ready to explore that idea. Not because it wasn't a possibility, but because of what it meant if it was true. There was no one in Okanisis with the ability or power to create such an interference, especially not Baz himself. Only one of the Old Ones would possess this kind of ultimate power, and while that was scary to Mandiba, it wasn't as scary as what the outcome would be. Why would one of the Old Ones work with a low-level imp like Baz? What did they stand to gain?

Mandiba opened his eyes and smashed his massive, stone-colored fist into the ground in front of him, destroying his carvings. He stood and gave one last look to the black moon before jumping to a lower ledge to make his way down the awful mountain. He was going to find Baz, that much he knew was true, but he was going to need to take a new approach. An approach that included an audience with the old Ones, but first, Mandiba needed to find out who his friends were.

B az smoked so much I'd gotten used to the constant, silver haze that hung throughout my apartment. His compulsion caused me to smoke more as well, which was probably why his insistent puffing didn't bother me anymore, but when I entered the building after killing Jack, something was different. The hall leading to my apartment was filled with nearly translucent smoke floating like ghostly apparitions passing through a haunted graveyard. There was so much smoke I was surprised it hadn't tripped the fire alarm, or at least riled up another tenant enough for them to call 911. My stomach dropped as I rushed down the hall to my door, afraid the tiny demon inside my apartment had actually set it on fire.

My hand shook as I struggled to put the key in the door. I turned it against the locking tumblers and threw it open, expecting the worst. It took a few seconds for my eyes and lungs to adjust to the smokescreen that greeted me, and while I could see there were no flames, my small apartment had taken on the look and smell of a packed pool hall at last call. Over in the direction of the kitchen counter I could see the glowing red cherry of Baz's cigarette bobbing up and down like a lightning bug flying through the deep fog of a starless night. I used the small fiery beacon to find my way to the counter where the outline of Baz became more and more visible the closer I got.

"Hey . . . man, what gives?" I struggled to ask, trying not to choke. "You gotta crack a window or something. My landlord is going to flip out over all this smoke and call the cops, which is the last thing we need to—"

Baz cut me off by holding one finger up, gesturing for me to be quiet. He plucked the cigarette from his mouth, dropped to the countertop, and ground it out on the piss-yellow Formica. Then he opened his mouth wide so his gaping maw took up most of the room on his face like when he'd pulled the poop amulet out of his throat. When his body had become more of an open mouth than anything else there was a sound like rushing wind, and I noticed the smoke being sucked toward the large orifice Baz was providing. When I realized he was actually inhaling all the smoke from the room, I didn't believe he'd be able to do it but I don't know why. It had only been a couple of days, but Baz had given me more than enough reason to not doubt his ability to perform outstanding feats.

The smoke flew into his mouth faster as the suction increased in power, to the extent that my hair and shirt flapped in the tremendous vacuum begging me to bend to its will. I stepped to the side so as not to be directly in front of him and closed my watering eyes against the whirlwind of smoke whipping by. A few seconds later the whooshing sound stopped and I opened my eyes, blinking against tears, to find the air completely cleared. I couldn't even smell the smoke anymore, which wasn't saying much since a lifetime of smoking had decimated my olfactory senses, but still the air seemed clean. More than that, it *was* clean. Fresh.

I rubbed my eyes with the heels of my hands and looked back down to Baz, whose mouth had returned to its normal size. He smirked and burped out a tiny puff of smoke, which he reached up into and pulled one of his cigarettes from before it evaporated into nothing. He lit it on his finger and screwed it into his mouth like it was the final brushstroke needed to complete a masterpiece. He inhaled deeply and spoke as he exhaled.

"Sorry about that," he said. "I guess I got a little carried away with the smoking, but you really scared me out there. I gotta say, I thought you were gonna fuck that one up. Way to adapt and think on your feet."

"Wait, what?" I asked. "How do you know how it went down? Can you see me, or something? I thought you were just able to tell that I did it because of the . . ."

I thrust my hand down the front of my shirt and pulled out the golden poop, which was now cool to the touch.

"Of course I can see you. What kind of question is that? Am I just supposed to take you at your word? That's not how this kind of thing goes down, okay. The amulet, like I said before, is necessary for the transference of energy. The energy that you create from your . . . deeds is channeled to me through it."

"Is that *all* it does?"

"Well . . . yeah, for the most part. At least, that's all you need to worry about it doing."

I didn't like the way Baz answered the question. It was like he was trying to hide something from me, and I took my hand off the amulet, letting it swing from the chain around my neck. I thought I felt a hint of heat coming off the thing again as it bounced lightly against my chest, but I ignored it, choosing to continue my focus on engaging Baz.

"How are you . . .? I mean, how can you . . .?"

"How am I able to see what you see? Is that what you're asking?"

"Well . . .yeah," I managed. "Are you like floating over my shoulder invisibly, or are you watching remotely through your crystal ball or something?"

"What do you think this is, *The Wizard of Oz*?" he asked incredulously. "We're connected now, my friend! That's how this whole arrangement works, or did you honestly not know that? I see what you see, I feel what you feel, and I know what you think. Got it?"

I wanted to feel angry, or outraged, or violated but for whatever reason I felt none of these things. As unsettling as it was to think I was connected to a hideously ugly blob of a being from another dimension, Baz was right. It did make sense. Instead of losing my cool and demanding to be cut loose from him, as I anticipated I would react, I instead nodded as I took it all in. I figured my subconscious already knew I wasn't in any position to argue and cut what would have been my initial reaction off at the pass.

"Okay, yeah," I said. "I got it."

"Good," Baz said flatly, materializing another cigarette from the ether, dropping the butt of the one currently in his mouth to the countertop, and replacing it without missing a beat.

"So, how'd I do out there?" I asked, suddenly starved for the approval of my magical partner in crime.

"You did great, kid," he said, smiling, the cigarette still stuck firmly in the corner of his mouth. "Scoping out the stop early was a great move, but I'm sure I don't have to tell you now that you should always have a backup plan. I honestly thought you were gonna bail when he walked up on you from the opposite direction, but you handled it like a champ. A real pro."

Champ? Pro? I'd be lying if I said my chest didn't slightly swell with pride as a reaction to Baz's comments. I'd never been a 'pro' at anything in my life, and certainly not to the extent that I or anyone else would consider me so. My job was mundane, mindless grunt-work at best that barely required a high school diploma let alone any sort of practiced and specialized skill to perform. Even so, I still conjured up some kind of demon-thing to help me excel at that. I'd never stuck with a hobby in my entire life, leaving behind a slew of unfinished model airplanes, half-assed watercolor paintings, and notes for a book I never started in the wake of my apathy.

Now, standing in front of me was a pint-sized creature of evil giving me the encouragement I never got in life that I never realized I needed. I was good at something now. I was a champ. Sure, the thing I was getting praise for was killing someone for my own selfish gain, but it was *something* and I was being told I was good at it. The reinforcement was all I needed to satiate my otherwise starved sense of ambition, and it propelled me to actually *want* to do better for Baz. For us.

"Thanks. Thank you," I finally managed. "So . . . does that mean everything went . . . according to plan?"

Baz smiled again, and I followed his eyes over to the phone just as it exploded in rings. I looked from the phone to Baz, and he raised his eyebrows, removing the cigarette temporarily from his mouth.

"Well?" he said, gesturing toward the ringing pile of plastic. "Ask not for whom the bell tolls, it tolls for thee, buddy."

I flew across the room, snatched the receiver from its cradle, and crammed it against my ear.

"Hello," I said, trying to sound casual through my heavy breaths. The jaunt across the small apartment was enough exertion to make me short of breath, and I silently cursed my lack of practiced cardio.

"Hi," came the female voice on the other end. "It's Liz."

She didn't have to say it since I knew it was her, but the fact that she referred to herself as 'Liz' sent goose bumps of excitement racing across my skin.

"Oh, hi, Liz," I said, getting my breathing under control. "What's up?"

That was dumb since I knew what was up. Her husband just died, and I killed him.

"I was just thinking about what you said to me earlier about if I needed someone to talk to."

"Oh yeah?" I tried not to sound excited, but found it hard to suppress.

"Yeah. I was wondering if you wouldn't mind if I came by your place for a while? You know, so we can . . . talk?"

I looked across the room to Baz who was still perched on the counter, smoking, but now he was giving me two enthusiastic, chubby little thumbs up.

"Uh . . . well yes," I finally answered. "Of course you can come over and talk."

It was just after four a.m. when the weight and sensation of something on my chest roused me from a hard sleep. The exhaustion from the energy I'd exerted for most of the night had taken its toll, and the last thing I wanted to do was open my eyes. A sharp poking at the center of my sternum persisted despite my attempts to ignore it. I opened my tired, heavy eyes and fought fatigue to focus on the sleeping face of Elizabeth lying next to me. There hadn't been much talking when she came over last evening, and in fact, the brief conversation and glass of wine turned into an all out animalistic sex-romp so seamlessly I thought I was dreaming, or possibly hallucinating. Seeing Elizabeth sleeping soundly next to me now brought back the memory of our heated passion from only hours ago, assuring me it was no dream.

"Hey! Come on, lover boy, wake up."

I turned my gaze from the face of an angel to see the hideous blob Baz standing on my chest, poking me with a fat finger over and over.

"Hey, I'm up okay," I whispered as consciousness took full hold of me now. "Be quiet! Don't . . . wake her."

"She can't hear or see me unless I want her to, so don't worry about that. Just get your ass up, and meet me in the kitchen."

Baz leapt from my chest to the mattress, then to the floor. I heard the burning crackle of his cigarette being lit as he plodded across my bedroom floor and out the door. I slipped from my bed slowly and as quietly as possible, trying not to disturb the sleeping beauty next to me, but she proved to be a heavy sleeper and barely moved at all. I found my boxer-briefs in the far corner of the room and slipped them on. I guess that's where they ended up last night in the frantic flurry of flying clothing as Elizabeth and I couldn't seem to get naked fast enough as our passion ignited.

I almost grabbed my robe from the hook on the back of the bedroom door, but changed my mind, deciding decency was not something I needed to worry about in front of my tiny demon friend. I trudged down the short hallway to the kitchen where Baz stood waiting and smoking. I didn't realize I was still wearing the golden poop around my neck until I caught a glimpse of its reflection in the toaster. Had I been wearing it through the entire marathon lovemaking session I'd just been through with Elizabeth? I guess, in the heat of the moment, I forgot to take it off.

"You have fun in there, big guy?" asked Baz, exhaling smoke through his smirk.

"Uh, yeah . . . I mean, it was great," I whispered. "Is that all you brought me out here for? Because I figured you'd know that seeing as how we're 'connected' and what not."

"Very funny, wise-ass," he said flatly while puffing his magic cigarette. "Now can the jokes, we've got work to do."

"Work? I don't have to even be at work for like five more hours. Can't we just deal with work in the—"

"Not your job, you idiot," interrupted Baz. "*Our* work. The kind of work that's gotten you this far, or have you forgotten about that already?"

It took me a few seconds to process what he was telling me, my brain still thick with sleep, but the look he was giving cleared away the cobwebs. A dark, heavy feeling pushed down on the lining of my stomach with a weight that threatened to break through. I wasn't sure I was ready to hear what Baz's definition of our *work* was.

"You know, now that you bring it up," I said with a put-on nonchalance, "I was gonna talk to you about it in the morning, but I think I'm all done, actually."

"You're all done? What do you mean by that?"

"Just that . . . you know, I got the promotion, I got the girl. I mean, I could be greedy, but that's really not my style, and I really appreciate everything you've done and—"

"Hold on," said Baz, holding his hand up to stop me.

He pulled another cigarette from the air, twisted it into his mouth, and produced another one that he handed to me. I didn't feel like smoking at the moment, but when the cigarette lit itself as I took it between my fingers I figured I shouldn't decline.

"First of all, before we go any further," he said, pacing in front of me on the counter, "you're not *all done*, okay. You're far from it in fact, my friend."

He paused to draw long and hard on his cigarette, and I took the opportunity to do the same to hide my mounting anxiety. The cherry burned bright and red as he inhaled, and the light reflected off his black orb eyes. At least I thought it was a reflection. Baz exhaled one of his trademarked, extra-large clouds of smoke before he continued.

"Yeah, you got the job and the girl, that's true, but this is not a 'happily ever after' kind of situation. Now comes the hard part, and that's maintenance, my friend."

"Maintenance?"

"Yeah, smart guy, maintenance. You can't just fuck off and expect to keep your job, or not put any work in building an actual relationship. At least not yet, you can't."

There was a slight snarl in Baz's voice I hadn't heard before, and I took another deep drag of my cigarette, not realizing I was clutching the gold poop medallion in my other hand.

"I guess I just thought—" I started.

"Well, you guessed wrong," Baz cut me off. "You're in for more work than you've ever had to do in your life, and I don't just mean at the office. The work will keep going when you get home, and have to deal with . . . her. Think about it. She's a beautiful woman who has grown accustomed to being provided a certain lifestyle, and you just pushed the provider of it under a bus."

Bile churned in my guts, and I could feel its familiar burning sensation working up my esophagus to the back of my throat. I sucked from my cigarette, hoping it would quell my urge to vomit, and the two things complemented each other like sewage in an open wound. I choked on the smoke, but was able to swallow the bile back down to its home before I composed myself to continue.

"I did my part, and . . . and . . ." My words sputtered and failed as I attempted to figure out where I was going with my thought.

"And I did mine." There was still a hint of snarl in Baz's voice as he mercifully interrupted my rambling. "I got you the stuff you wanted just like I said I would, but that's as far as it goes. You didn't think you could get a promotion, dick off all day, and still collect a check, did you? And what about sleeping beauty in there? Did you think she would all of a sudden become a brain-dead Stepford wife or something?"

I dropped my eyes and slowly shook my head even though I had secretly hoped that's how it would be; money for nothing, and my chicks for free. In hindsight, it was ignorantly optimistic of me to apply eighties rock lyrics to real life situations even when magic and otherworldly creatures are involved.

"Exactly," continued Baz, the sharp edge in his voice now dulled into obscurity. "This is why we've got work to do. We have to keep working together so that you can 'maintain' your new life. So we both can."

"Both? What's that even supposed to mean?" I asked sharply. "Just because we're 'connected' or whatever you've been getting your jollies off to me getting mine?"

"What? No! Well, sometimes but that's not the point here. Remember when I told you that you killing people here boosts my 'street-cred' back home? Well, that's mostly true, and pretty soon it can boost me up so high I'll never have to go back to those streets ever again."

"What do you mean by 'mostly'?"

"Alright, listen up, kid," said Baz, grasping yet another cigarette from thin air. "We don't have much time, so I'll give you the short version."

Mandiba thought better of going straight to the Old Ones with the problems he had encountered in attempting to track Baz. On his way down the steep, sharp ledges of Okanisis's black mountain he'd decided taking that approach might facilitate further difficulties in his search. He hated the idea that one of the Old Ones may be helping Baz and tried to put it out of his mind while he brainstormed other hypotheses, but regardless of his effort, the thought continued to swirl around in his head.

If one of the Old Ones were using their power to help Baz, what did they have to gain from it? The rules of their realm had been set in place eons ago, and as far as he knew, breaking them hadn't been attempted since Mephistopheles failed in his arrogant attempt back in the dark ages, yet now Baz seemed to be doing the impossible. He didn't have the power, ability, or clearance to pass through to Earth even if some human had harnessed a limited amount of magic to summon him. But, Baz was there despite this limitation, and now was attempting to make it so he never had to come back.

Mandiba couldn't help thinking that Baz was more than likely a pawn working for someone who doled out power to him in single-serving sizes in order to further a much larger, and more important, plan. Mandiba leapt from one ledge to the next, quickly approaching the ground, when he was struck with another thought he hadn't yet considered. What if Baz wasn't working with anyone? While he thought it to be very unlikely, if it was true it meant a lowly imp had found some way to circumvent centuries of magical laws all on his own.

It was a scary thought because it meant he'd be dealing with something he'd never encountered before, and if the Old Ones weren't helping Baz achieve this it probably meant they wouldn't be able to help Mandiba stop him. He jumped from the final outcropping of sharp stone, landed at the base of the mountain, and slid the rest of the way to the ground on his feet, steadying himself with one hand on the ground behind him. He took one last look up at the black moon before setting out through the treacherous Okanisis terrain. He was going to need help, this much was true, but not from the Old Ones. Mandiba was going to have to pay a visit to someone he'd hoped he would never have to see, but as far as he could tell he didn't have much of a choice.

12

I lay in bed next to the still sleeping Elizabeth, and even though I still had a couple hours before I would even need to think about getting up I couldn't go back to sleep. All I could do was stare at the ceiling, trying to process the conversation I'd just had with Baz. I clutched the golden poo amulet I was still wearing, which worked to strangely comfort me. I couldn't believe I thought this would be so easy, so cut and dry. Of course I'd have to work hard to maintain not only my promotion, but also my job in general. As far as the Elizabeth situation was concerned, I had clearly been short-sighted and naïve. The hard part was out of the way, sure. I mean, I had her interest now even though I'm sure she didn't know why she was interested, but she wasn't just some toy I could play with and put back on the shelf when I was done. At least not yet anyway, but to be honest, I wasn't even sure if that was what I wanted.

Actually, who was I kidding? Of course that was exactly what I wanted. If it wasn't I wouldn't be lying here right now trying to come up with a plan for the day. Baz was quite clear the killing must continue, and each one would come with a reward facilitated by Baz through transference of energy to him from the golden turd around my neck. I asked him why I couldn't just include the whole kit and caboodle of things into just one killing, but Baz had sternly told me it didn't work like that.

I didn't understand his explanation completely, but it had to do with the amount of energy produced by my actions in relation to the amount needed to garner the desired result. There was one silver lining Baz pointed out to me during his longwinded diatribe, which was the more killings I did, the stronger he would become. I didn't ask at the time, but I guessed this was what Baz meant by us *both* maintaining our new lives. This would allow him to produce even larger wishes as well as other added benefits he wouldn't elaborate on, but assured me would benefit the both of us.

"Look, I know this may not seem like the most ideal situation," Baz had said, "but if we stop now you'll be fucked. Not only will you eventually end up losing Elizabeth and your job, but you will most certainly end up in an unimaginably worse place than you were before we started our little . . . relationship."

I had more questions rattling around in my head than I could count, but I asked none of them. Instead, I chose complacency and said only that I understood. Baz was clearly affected by my agreeableness, and his tone and energy softened as he continued.

"I'm not going to pretend that killing people to facilitate your desires is a . . . easy thing to do," he said to me. "At least not yet, but it *will* become that way for you soon enough."

When Baz said this it made me wonder just how connected we truly were, because if he were able to share in my experiences he would know this wasn't true. It was already easy for me. I knew I'd only done it twice, and the whole act of murder was completely new to me, but it just felt so easy. Baz had said it himself I was a pro. Another thing to consider was that Baz did indeed know exactly how I felt already, and was just trying to psych me up, or psych me out, or something. The flipside was we were connected in some aspects, but not all, which would mean the entire 'connection' trip he'd laid on me was complete horseshit. I chose not to believe the latter possibility for two reasons: I didn't want to think Baz could be manipulating me for his own gain, and I didn't want to believe I could be so manipulated.

Baz had sent me back to bed after our talk, citing I should get some rest while I could because I would need to be sharp and focused for our next kill, which would be taking place that day. I couldn't afford to miss another day of work, especially since my next victim was to be my boss, Mr. Johansson. The golden poop, still clutched tightly in my hand, grew warm as I thought about how I was going to go about my task in a few hours. I finally drifted off into a deep sleep for the next two hours until my alarm went off like a pistol signaling my start into a new day.

I was surprised how natural it felt to wake up with Elizabeth and comingle our morning routines as we went about preparing for the day. I was getting ready to go to work while she was getting ready to go to the funeral parlor, which was understandable seeing as a bus crushed her husband less than twenty-four hours ago. Hopefully sooner rather than later we'd both be getting ready for work together while deciding which of my mix tapes to listen to on the drive in to work. *Classic, Alt-Prog, Death-Grind Love Songs that Start with the Letter 'G', Ultra, Super, Retro Classic Glass-Core,* or *Noise-Stomp Sympathy Ballads: Songs From the Smash Broadway Musical.* Every day would be an adventure.

Elizabeth shook me from my fantasy when she went to leave, but stopped to tell me she had a good feeling about us, and how she knew how odd and callous that sounded given the present circumstance, but she also made it clear she was coming back after the wake tonight so we could 'talk' about her new 'feelings'.

If I had somehow managed to work up to a point in my life where I would actually be having this exact conversation with Elizabeth without the intervention of magic, evil or otherwise, I would have been elated. I would've done anything to talk to Liz about her feelings, especially if they involved me, but now since this reaction was merely a byproduct of the die I cast it no longer held its shiny appeal. It didn't matter anyway, because I was never going to have that conversation.

After I killed Mr. Johansson there wouldn't be any need, because the concerns she felt were so important they needed to be communicated to me would be wiped clean, never to concern her again. I told Baz I'd rather focus on Liz first so I could put her on autopilot, so to speak, while I put face time in at work pretending to learn my new responsibilities until I could kill them away.

I knew it seemed like I should be doing things the other way around, but for me it was better this way. I'd never been good at relationships, and after Baz reminded me of the workload they entailed, a small snowball of panic began to roll down the side of my brain well on its way to doubling and tripling in size. No, I couldn't trust myself to deal with Liz without intervention on Baz's part, at least for the time being.

I promised myself once I got things balanced at work with my new position I would cash in my kills for magical work-related needs only. Then I could use my time to focus on Liz with the hope we could one day reach a place where I wouldn't have to keep slipping her the proverbial mickey via demon-magic. I'd slowly wean us both off our dependency on Baz and actually be happy and in love for real. It sounded good in my head when I thought about how it would all work out that way, but the fantasy didn't last long. I don't know who I was kidding with that *happy and in love* stuff. What did that even mean? It didn't matter because, at least for the foreseeable future, I needed Baz and he needed me. Now it was just a race to see who wouldn't *need* the other first. That was when the trouble would start.

No time to think about that now anyway, especially not if Baz was constantly reading my thoughts, although I didn't believe I was thinking anything he didn't already know. I went back over part of our conversation from last night where Baz explained what our next *move* for tomorrow would be. He told me with great conviction I needed to kill Mr. Johansson for several reasons, each more convincing than the last.

"Sure, you can just kill some shmuck on your way to the office, or on your lunch break, but that would be such a waste. If you kill your boss it's like a double-down, triple word score. Not only will I be able to do my part, which as we agreed would be to ensure things keep going nice and smooth with you and Liz, but you would help make your transition much easier by causing a sudden vacated position of power, thus taking all focus off you completely. You could probably just fuck off, and go home after lunch every day for at least a few weeks. It's really worth it for that alone when you think about it."

He was right too. Killing Mr. Johansson would make my life easier in both of its new developments, with magic taking care of one thing, and the chaos created to make that magic happen taking care of the other. It was worth it.

I glanced at my watch and cursed myself for getting wrapped up in my own thoughts because now I was going to have to really hustle if I was going to make my bus.

14

Mandiba had experienced a thousand times worse than anything Okanisis had to offer since he came into existence, but that didn't mean he cared for the place much. The favor he'd curried with the Old Ones during the restructuring gave him permanent citizenship, along with nearly the run of the place. He had immunity when it came to most of the laws decreed by the Old Ones, but only most. They hadn't survived longer than time itself without knowing what they were doing. They gave Mandiba just enough power to make him dangerous, but keep him loyal.

The Old Ones also displayed their powerful influence by making an example of someone who pushed them too far. Someone who flew too close to the sun on wings of wax and still spit in the gods' eyes as he crashed to the ground. This was who Mandiba had traveled halfway across the hot side of Okanisis to the black pits to find. Mephistopheles. Mandiba knew it wasn't a good idea, but it was less risky than cluing in an all-powerful being that you were on to them going rogue. Mandiba hoped he was wrong about that, but he couldn't rule anything out.

The pits were understood to be off limits, as it was widely known as a place of punishment you wouldn't want to visit voluntarily, but Mandiba was exempt from that rule. Now he stood before three great holes that comprised the awful place, waiting to be greeted, as he knew he would be. The three pits were roughly the same diameter, arranged in a pseudo-triangle shape with six or so feet of dusty, burnt ground between them. The three great holes were filled with a rolling blackness that lacked the consistency of liquid, but was decidedly thicker than air. The blackness rolled off the sides of the pits like weightless waves, and what wasn't re-claimed into the pit evaporated like wisps of smoke. Mandiba watched the blackness roll and rise from the pits like three giant boiling cauldrons in silence and wondered if his trip had been a waste. He'd never actually had contact with Mephistopheles before, but knew he had been banished to the pits to remain shackled to their depths for eternity.

Suddenly Mandiba felt what would be imperceptible to most inhabitants of Okanisis. It wasn't a rumble or a quake, but more of a hum, a vibration signaling that the one he sought was near. The psychic energy was coming from the pit he was standing closest to, and a moment later blackness rose from the center of it, obscuring what had risen out with it, but Mandiba knew who it was. The dark smokescreen dripped from the form it was concealing back down into the pit, revealing a thin-framed, human-like creature with skin as white as the well-fitting three piece suit he wore. It was Mephi-stopheles.

Mephistopheles floated with a graceful smoothness from the air above the pit over to the ground in front of his visitor. As he got closer, Mandiba could see tiny white horns poking up from either side of his forehead, which flanked his slicked back, silver hair. Mandiba knew Mephistopheles chose to appear in this form due to his affinity for the Earthly realm he was almost able to escape to. He purposely wanted to look how humans deemed demons and devils to look because he enjoyed the power it gave him to hold over them. A power they unknowingly provided him with as a re-sult of fear they felt from their own fabricated folklore and legends. Mandiba personally thought he looked foolish in this form, as he found the human interpretation of them as 'demons' to be some-where between insulting and laughable. Humans' predisposition to fear anything they didn't understand was just one of the many things on a long list of reasons he found them to be deplorable. He simply didn't understand the value Mephistopheles saw in living amongst them, but he hoped the old creature's unique knowledge would help him find Baz.

"Hello Mandiba," said Mephistopheles in a pitch perfect human tone. "I knew you would come."

15

I got to work early. Like, two hours early. I left hot on the heels of Liz, not wanting to waste any time dawdling around my apartment since I didn't have any kind of plan on how I was going to 'handle' Mr. Johansson. Conveniently though, I had an idea not one second after I'd plopped down on the bus. I clutched at my chest, checking for the sixth or seventh time I had the golden poop medallion. It was there just like it had been the last times, buried beneath my undershirt, dress shirt, and sweater-vest.

I wouldn't be able to use the buses this time because I couldn't picture my big shot boss taking public transportation. I imagined he drove some kind of mid-level luxury sedan, and even if I knew which in the packed parking garage it was, I doubt I could push him under the tires of his own car. No, that was stupid. The idea I had on the bus, however, was not stupid. Mr. Johansson was a real health nut and was always finding idiotic ways to exercise around the office. He sat on one of those exercise balls at his desk, had a chin up bar in his office, and walked up the twelve flights of steps to the office every morning wearing a weighted vest.

I found this last one out while lurking about the stairwells one morning looking for a spot to smoke a pre-work joint. I was just about to light up when I heard a strange noise coming up from the stairs below me, and I thought some lunatic was strangling a cat. It turned out the sound was just the labored breathing of Mr. Johansson reaching the end of his torturous, self-imposed, morning constitutional. I pocketed the joint and greeted him, receiving a grunt and nod in return.

Since then, I've seen him enter the office through the stairwell door every morning at 8:58 a.m. dripping in sweat and wearing his goofy orange weighted vest. My plan was to slip into the stairwell at 8:55, hide around the corner of his final turn, and push him down the steps. I knew it wasn't fool proof, but I figured if I gave him a hard shove the momentum mixed with the added weight of his vest would bring him down hard enough on his head to get the job done. Now I only had to find a way to pass the hour and twenty-two minutes I had left before it was time to make my move.

I busied myself with filling out the paperwork necessary for my promotion, but that only ate up fifteen minutes. I spent the next hour and seven minutes sitting at my desk anxiously trying to not appear anxious. I pretended to look over documents that were to comprise my day's work, but I couldn't concentrate and was retaining none of what I read. The words ran together, changing into nothing more than blobs of foreign shapes, making it feel like I was staring into a bottomless stack of Rorschach tests rather than sales documents. I mimed stapling pieces of paper together for around ten minutes or so, taking great care to make sure I appeared rapt in my task. I even made sure to affix a scowl to my face that would communicate my dissatisfaction with having to perform such a mindless, yet necessary duty. Around ten minutes into this little scene I was struck with a thought that gave me pause. What was my backup plan?

I all of a sudden realized how many variables were at play with my current plan that could potentially throw the train off the fucking tracks. What if today Mr. Johansson arrived just three minutes earlier than usual? He would walk right in the door before I would have a chance to meet him in the stairwell. Or, what if today happened to be the day he beat his normal time because he really wanted to push himself? Or, what if he called in sick today? What if he decided to take the elevator today? What if? What if? What if?

Baz had been so impressed with how I thought on my feet when my plan was thrown off yesterday, but could I pull it off if things went pear-shaped again today? The hair on my neck and arms stood on end in the uncomfortable way that happens when you're trying to keep from shitting yourself. The golden poop was warm against my chest, but not in the comforting way I was used to. The heat it produced now was uncomfortable while edges I hadn't felt before scratched evidence of their existence into my sensitive, pale skin.

I started sweating, partly due to the discomfort the medallion was currently causing me and partly because my mind was racing to come up with a backup plan. I had nothing. My synapses weren't firing fast enough to come up with an alternative 'kill plan'. Goddammit, why couldn't Mr. Johansson just take the goddamned bus like everyone else? I pushed back a few inches from my desk so I could see past the short cubicle walls, hoping to catch a glimpse of something that would inspire the beginning of a backup plan. A backup plan I had become consumed with coming up with. My eyes darted with the frantic nervousness of someone who was trying to get away with something.

In my quick scan of the office I saw a fire extinguisher, a large rubber trash can, a small metal trash can, and the copy machine. In theory it would make sense that you could put these four objects together in some type of deadly fashion. Unfortunately, I didn't have the time or mental capacity to do that. I was going to have to just hope my original plan worked without a hitch, because I was running out of time to formulate a proper back up. The time in the bottom right corner of my computer monitor said 8:54 a.m., which meant I only had a minute or so before I needed to be in position on the stairwell.

The gold poop suddenly burned extra hot against my chest, and I suppressed a yelp of pain by biting the heel of my palm. As I grabbed at my chest to pull the hot metal away from my skin I was struck with a thought. Mr. Johansson walks through the door at exactly 8:58 am, but when the office clock says 8:58 and not the clock on my computer. The office clock was exactly four minutes faster than my computer, and as my legs worked to propel me to my feet, I whipped my head around to the stairwell door just in time to see it begin to open.

16

I knew you would come.

Mephistopheles' words echoed in Mandiba's head as he struggled to determine what the banished, human-lover was talking about. At first he thought he might have foolishly walked himself into a trap and tensed in preparation for the possible impending attack. Mandiba searched Mephistopheles' face for signs of aggression and was surprised to find the demon's human face relaxed, smiling, and overall calm. Mandiba allowed himself to relax, but only slightly, still unsure of the banished one's intentions. He looked around before he spoke and struggled to see through the black mist rising off the pits, trying to ensure they were indeed alone.

"It's okay, Mandiba," said Mephistopheles. "I can assure you we are quite alone. The Old Ones made sure of that when they banished me here. No one in Okanisis has the ability to access my new . . . home. Frankly, I'm surprised you were able to come to me. The Old Ones must value you highly to bestow such power and favor upon you, but then again, I imagine that puts you firmly under their thumb."

Mephistopheles put his hands behind his back and began to

pace. Each step he took burned a smoking black footprint in the rusty dirt around the pit. Mandiba did not take kindly to his comment and began to smolder inside like the footprints being made around him. He didn't like Mephistopheles' idea that he was just a puppet on a string for the Old Ones to make dance at their slightest whim. The human looking, banished one stopped his pacing and looked Mandiba in the eyes quizzically, waiting for his reply and, after another moment, it came.

"How is it you knew I would come?" he asked. "And since you know so much, what is it you think I came here for?"

"Well, well, well," chuckled Mephistopheles, "I guess I expected someone like you to know more about me. Especially since you're here now."

"No one knows anything about you truly," answered Mandiba. "The Old Ones have all but blotted out your existence entirely throughout Okanisis. You exist only in whispered legends and half-truths told by mature beings struggling to hold on to a memory they're not even sure is real. Not me though. I know you. I know everything about you."

"That certainly is flattering to hear, my new friend, and while I don't doubt you know a great deal about me, you don't know as much as you think."

A glint of red flashed in his eyes, which unsettled Mandiba for only a moment before he stilled himself against the unfamiliar feeling of . . . fear. The thought that he might be walking into a trap presented itself again, and he broke eye contact to scan the pits behind Mephistopheles again. His eyes darted back and forth, landing once again on Mephistopheles' ominous, unblinking eyes. He was shaking his head, disappointed.

"I told you we were alone, but I understand your mistrust of me. I would feel the same way if I were you, I suppose. That being said, allow me the opportunity to earn your trust by telling you what I know. There's been another escape from Okanisis in the same vein as my own so many years ago. The escapee has no business leaving here for any period of time regardless of the length, but has done so anyway, breaking several of the laws put in place to stop such a thing. Of course the Old Ones want the offender back, and have called upon the one they've granted the ability to do so.

"That is you, and congratulations on such a prestigious position. Something's wrong though. He's out there, but you can't find him. He's interfering with your tracking ability somehow, but that makes no sense to you, does it? This particular escapee lacks the capacity for such a power as that, let alone the ability to leave Okanisis. Nothing is right about this situation, and now you are concerned you've been double-crossed. Set up. Betrayed. Am I right, my new friend?"

Mandiba was shocked by what Mephistopheles was telling him, but he kept his face stern and expressionless, unsure of his next move. The fact he knew so much about why Mandiba had come to him gave him reason to believe he was possibly a part of the conspiracy surrounding Baz. He was already here though and had no other choice but to ask Mephistopheles for his help. He just hoped he wasn't being distracted into wasting time by being sent on a wild goose chase, or worse.

"That's very impressive," said Mandiba. "It seems like you know everything about the situation I am in, and I'm sure you also know I am here to ask for your help, but how is it you know all these things?"

Mephistopheles threw back his head and released a loud, stuttered laughter that sounded like a rifle report as it echoed around the pits.

"You really don't know a lot about me," he said. "My friend, I know these things because I have seen them. I saw this happen back when it was I who was attempting my escape, which is why I don't blame you for seeking my help. I'm afraid it won't help much though."

"And why is that?"

"Because, among other things, I have seen how this plays out."

17

It wasn't even 11 a.m. and I was on the bus heading home already. This was the longest amount of time I'd spent at work in the last three days, so I guess you could call it the first day of my promotion. I did fill out all the paperwork, after all. Our entire office was sent home due to the overwhelming shock and sadness we all felt from having lost our dear, beloved boss, Mr. Johansson. The three floors below us were also cleared out and sent home for the day, but that was because the intrusiveness of the investigation would be a disruption to their workday.

The reason the authorities needed to investigate in and around those floors was because Mr. Johansson tumbled down three whole flights of steps before crumbling into a pile of cartoonish limbs all bent the wrong way on a landing. Apparently, on his way down, Mr. Johansson left quite a trail, with chunks of flesh and viscera along the way. I overheard one of the officers remarking to another about how poor Mr. Johansson had landed on his head at just the right angle and with just the right force to crack his skull all the way around to his eye socket and shoot his eyeball straight out of his head. They said it must have popped out and flew off behind him because they found it smashed like a pus-filled grape on the second landing. The once sparkling baby blue cornea now floated dulled and unfocused in the quickly spreading ocular fluid. He had landed on it as he continued to fall.

It was my guess he was dead by the time he'd smashed his own eyeball, although there was no way I could be sure. I'm in no way an expert on the damage a human skull can take before having to throw in the towel, but I just had this feeling. It was an odd electrical sensation, not like I was getting shocked, but how it feels just after you do. I felt it just after barreling through the stairwell door and plowing my lowered shoulder into Mr. Johansson's midsection. He flew up and back, nearly going head over heels, as his head caught the fifth step down with what I perceived to be a deafening crack, his neck bending to the side at an unnatural angle.

The feeling started in my chest at the familiar spot where the amulet touched. Time seemed to slow as a voice in my head screamed *don't stop running*, and I continued up the stairs as Mr. Johansson continued to fall down them. I took the stairs two and three at a time, keeping my pace and breathing even until I reached the eighteenth floor. I stood on the landing, caught my breath, and listened for any commotion floating up from the floors below. There was only the low whir of air passing through ductwork that cut through parts of the stairwell, and nothing else.

I cracked open the door and peeked out to see the hallway was clear. I stepped out, closing the door gently so as not to make a sound, and casually walked to the elevator. I took it down to the first floor, walked outside, and headed down the block to get a cup of coffee. Eight minutes later I was back on the elevator heading up to my office floor. I strolled in and nodded to the receptionist who hadn't been there when I came in originally so, in her eyes, I was only just arriving. Everything seemed to be business as usual so far, meaning no one had discovered Mr. Johansson, which I hoped also meant no one had seen me sprint from my chair and ram the slightly open stairwell door like a blitzing linebacker.

The office was much fuller than when I'd gotten there hours earlier, but still missing a considerable amount of staff who would no doubt be trickling in over the next fifteen or twenty minutes. I strolled down the rows of cubicles with a nonchalance you wouldn't expect from someone who just killed their boss. I sat at my desk, sipped my coffee, pretended to check emails with great interest, and waited.

It wasn't anyone from our office, or even from our floor, that finally found Mr. Johansson exactly fifty-seven minutes after I'd sat down at my desk. The wail of approaching sirens prompted the nosey and easily distracted to look out the west-facing window. They called others over to join them when they saw the collection of assorted emergency vehicles lining up in front of the building. They pointed and gasped as police, firemen, and paramedics sprinted from their vehicles and into the building. A panic-wave rippled through the office as people began to wonder if they were in danger and should evacuate.

As if on cue the phone at the receptionist desk rang, and Nancy answered with a concern her southern twang could not mask. She didn't talk much to the person on the other end, but mostly listened with widening eyes and a hand over her mouth. A moment later she dropped the phone back into the cradle and stood at her desk, silent and stunned. After a few seconds she burst into tears and retreated to the ladies' room with a fellow female co-worker in tow. A few random phones rang across the office with the calls from gossip-craving, building-busybodies from various other floors. Some had already heard and some were asking as if we knew, but eventually enough pieces of the puzzle were put together just in time for several police officers to arrive at our office and tell everyone what I already knew.

The detective, who rounded up the entire office so he could address everyone at once, said what happened appeared to be an accident but they couldn't rule anything out pending investigation. He told us he understood what a shock something like this was and suggested a few local outreach programs if anyone felt like they needed to talk to someone. He said we would each need to give a brief statement and could then leave.

And brief they were. It seemed like annoying busywork to the officer I talked to who, along with his colleagues, didn't think anything useful would come out of talking to us. I imagined they either already believed they had a solid lead, or they already believed it was an accident. Whatever the reason, it was clear the officers felt they were wasting their time talking to us. The questions they asked came in the form of bare-boned sentences whose few words felt like grunts being spat rather than spoken from the mouths of these pigs.

The entire battery included: name, official job title, did you see anything out of the ordinary this morning, and what was your contact info. They originally asked the first few lined up to get out of the office what time they had arrived that morning, but they nixed that question when the detective in charge told them they could get that information from the timestamp on the security video, and to also *hurry these people along*. My blood froze in my veins and black spots danced around my field of vision as I struggled for a moment to not blackout. Security video? Of course there was a security video! Just because no one was around in the office to see me didn't mean the great eye in the sky didn't capture my every move. I had to get home to Baz, and fast. I answered the officer's questions with a gruffness that challenged his own and brushed past him after the final digit of my phone number was off my lips.

The bus jerked to a stop and I exited, pulling my phone from my pocket to silence the fourth call in a row from Elizabeth. The only person, well *thing* really, that I could talk to then was Baz, and I needed to talk to him immediately. I shoved my phone back in my pocket and began the four-block walk from the bus stop to my building. The walk felt longer then it ever had before.

" **A**nswer your phone," said Baz as I burst into my apartment on the verge of a complete anxiety attack.

He was standing on the kitchen counter where he usually 'held court' during our conversations, and as per the usual, he was smoking. Judging from the thick wisps of smoke hovering in and around the kitchen it would be fair to guess it was one of many he'd been smoking. I slammed the door and bounded toward him, telegraphing my panic with my eyes.

"Hey, we've got a big—" but that was all I could say before Baz interrupted me.

"I said, answer your phone." His tone was stern but not angry, and he drew deeply on his cigarette, motioning with his free hand for me to *get on with it already.*

I pulled the phone from my pocket, not even realizing it had been vibrating. From the looks of it, it hadn't stopped since I got off the bus. According to the backlit screen I had just missed the twenty-fourth call from Elizabeth, and the twenty-fifth was coming in now.

"It's Elizabeth," I said. "I'll call her back in a few minutes but right now I really have to talk to you."

"I know that. I understand and appreciate the urgency of the situation, but right now I need you to answer your phone," he replied calmly.

"But . . ."

"You've just killed three people in three days for this girl. Answer your goddamn phone!"

The urge to continue arguing subsided, and I relented to Baz's request.

"Hello," I finally said into the phone.

"Oh my darling," came Elizabeth's sweet voice into my ear. "I've been trying to get ahold of you. I was so worried."

"Oh yeah, sorry about that. There was . . . something happened at work."

"I called there looking for you first, and Nancy told me that something awful had happened and everyone was sent home. I asked if you were okay, and when she said yes I hung up without finding out what she was talking about. I don't care what it was as long as you're okay."

The tender concern and care in Elizabeth's voice, while fabricated by magic, still felt good, making me temporarily forget about my current problem.

"Oh yeah, I'm fine. It's just that—"

"Good! I'm so relieved. Anyway, my darling, the reason I was calling you originally was to tell you to forget about what I said earlier about new feelings, and having to talk about them. I can't remember what my concerns were now, or why I even had them. I just want to be with you. I'm sorry I'm stuck at this boring funeral parlor all day, but I'll be out of here and home to you just as soon as I can. Okay?"

"Uh, yeah . . . okay. Sounds good."

Elizabeth made a sound into the phone like she may have wanted to blow me a kiss, but instead deep throated the receiver. She hung up, and I set the phone on the counter next to the smug, smiling Baz. He was certainly efficient, I had to say that much, but part of me did feel strange about Liz sprinting from the casket of her recently dead husband and into my arms. I couldn't complain though, it was what I wanted.

"What'd I tell ya?" asked Baz, still smiling. "No muss, no fuss, and no discussions about feelings or concerns. I told you I'd get you started off right."

"Yeah you did, and that's great," I said, slowly returning to my senses, "but we have a potential problem. A big potential problem."

"Yeah, yeah, yeah," he said dismissively. "The cameras. I know all about it."

Of course he did, we were 'connected', according to him. I allowed myself to relax for a moment before replying.

"Okay, good," I said, "so you know then?"

"Yep."

"And, you already took care of it?"

"Nope."

My heart sank, and I was starting to feel how I did back at the office when I found out about the cameras.

"No?" I finally managed.

"No, but I sure can. I can make it so there's not a trace of you on that video until you came back in the second time with your coffee."

"Good!" I said a little louder than I should have. "Do it then! Take me off it."

"No problem, my friend, but you know what I'm gonna need to make that happen."

The rusty metal door that granted access to the roof of my building closed behind me, grinding across the cement step. The sound was like someone dropped an armload of pots and pans down the stairs and it echoed all around for several seconds before decaying into nothingness, leaving me standing in the silence of the dark stairwell. It was at this moment I was struck with the thought that maybe my relationship with Baz was moving a little too quickly.

This was my fourth kill in three days. My third was less than eight hours ago, but Baz was insistent. He seemed different too, like he was nervous. Maybe not nervous, but he was definitely on edge. The sense of urgency in his voice was far greater than it had been when discussing the previous kills. I decided to chalk it up to the fact that we had to act fast before the security tapes were viewed from my office, but still something was . . . off.

He already knew Ms. McNeese was on the roof tending to her 'garden', as she called it. It was really just a dozen or so things she had planted in individual pots, but she took great pride in the care she gave to them and never missed a day. Her garden consisted of roses, tomatoes, tulips, bell peppers, a rubber tree, and basil. She was a harmless old coot, but people in the building did worry about her being up on the roof by herself, especially since she would move many of her plants to the ledge daily to catch what she called 'that good sun.'

I thought it seemed like a waste, having to use up a kill on something so utilitarian as removing my image from the video. It was like buying tires. Sure you *need* them for safety, but there is no joy or fun to be gained from the hundreds you shell out. You can't fuck them, or snort them, or smoke them, but most painfully large expenditures on necessities leave you with an empty, 'ripped off' feeling. Only when it's pouring rain, you slam on your brakes, and are able to stop without sliding off the road into a tree or ditch do you appreciate the money you spent on those tires. I guess this was my way of making an investment to keep from crashing into a ditch.

I wanted to take a moment to process and decompress but Baz was intent on me doing this now. I'm no expert on otherworldly magic so I have no scope of the intricacies of Baz's timing and could only go along with what he said. My hope was that even if the police had already watched the video and seen me on it, Baz would be able to use his power to change not only the video, but also their minds and memories. This was my reply to Baz in hopes of buying a little more time between my kills, but he shot me down and a minute later I was on my way up to the roof.

When I stepped out into the light I had to squint against the harsh brightness until my eyes adjusted and I was able to see again. The first object that came into view was the rumpled, pudgy figure of Ms. McNeese standing at the ledge with her back toward me as she arranged her plants for optimal sun exposure. She was wearing the usual khaki-colored top and capri pants that showed off the lumpy, vein-covered flesh of her lower legs. I'm sure during her youth her features were soft and delicate, but age had turned those times into distant memories, taking away what were once thin and defined ankles and turning them into the shapeless, stumpy 'can-kles' I saw before me.

She was wearing a sunhat that matched her outfit and oversized sunglasses that covered the sides of her face as well. They looked more like a pair of welder's safety glasses than casual, sun-deflecting eyewear. She was only fifteen feet in front of me, but hadn't noticed I was there, directing her full attention to her precious plants and their arrangement on the ledge. I closed the door slowly and quietly and stood there for a few seconds to make sure she wasn't going to turn around. Then, I went for it. I offered no warning and gave myself no time to second guess or even savor what I was doing. I broke into a full sprint from my standing position, lowered my shoulder, and buried it into Ms. McNeese's back between her ribs and kidney on her left side. I was surprised at how little resistance her body gave, and it felt like I had just cross-checked a giant bag of marshmallows.

The next few seconds went by in a blur. The force of my shoulder's impact into her soft lumpy body was more than enough to send her over the ledge, careening face first toward the sidewalk below. I had barely seen her feet disappear before redirecting my momentum back toward the door. If Ms. McNeese made any kind of sound as she fell I certainly couldn't hear it standing in the darkened stairwell. I stayed there waiting to hear something, but either the stone walls of the corridor kept the sound out or there hadn't been anything to hear yet. I figured I wouldn't be able to hear the actual impact of her flabby body from all the way in the stairwell, but thought I would at least be able to hear screams of people on the street who had just witnessed what I'm sure was an explosively gore-filled impact.

My head started swimming and I felt woozy until the familiar warmth of the poop medallion burned hot against my chest. I clutched at it, feeling the rising heat in my hand despite the cotton barrier my t-shirt provided, and I was instantly calm. I also snapped to the thought that I needed to get the hell out of the stairwell. If people were indeed congregating around the puddle of blood, bone, and blubber that was Ms. McNeese—and I was sure they were—the last place I needed to be seen was coming out of the hallway that granted residents roof access.

If I was spotted and the police questioned people in the building, it wouldn't be long before I would be suspected, and I'm sure it would cost another kill for Baz to absolve me of this crime as well. If I wasn't careful, this whole relationship was going to turn into a 'robbing Peter to pay Paul'-type situation and that was a vicious cycle I wanted no part of. I just needed to do this so I wouldn't be on the security tapes anymore, then I could go back to the plan of living happily ever after with Elizabeth while having everything else I could ever want in life.

The gold poop burned warmer in my hand, urging me to press on and stop dawdling. I skipped the rest of the way down the steps, taking them two and three at a time until I came to the door leading back into the hallway of the building. I reached for the doorknob with my free hand when a surge of intense heat shot from the medallion, burning the hand that held it to my chest. It was so much hotter than I'd ever felt before. I let go of the doorknob and dropped to my knees. Just as quickly as it came, the heat was gone and, as I used the banister to pull myself up, I heard voices.

I held my breath as I heard the exasperated tone of several tenants running past the door I was just about to walk out of. I couldn't tell exactly what they were saying, but their tone told me they'd discovered what happened to Ms. McNeese. The medallion had warned me. It was actually helping me not get caught. I stood up without making a sound, touched the doorknob again with one hand, and wrapped the other around the gold poop. It was still warm, but as the voices faded in the distance it began to cool. I slowly turned the knob, waited another second, and opened the door to an empty hallway.

I stepped out and closed the door slower than I opened it so not even the slightest click was audible. I hurried over to the elevator, jammed the button to summon it, and as the numbers dinged indicating the steel box of salvation was approaching, I prayed it would be unoccupied. My hand was up my shirt now, clutching the medallion to make sure it wasn't trying to warn me of anything again, but the only warmth being generated was my own body heat from the death grip I had on the thing. At last the illuminated numbers above told me the elevator was here, and I held my breath as the silver doors slid apart. I exhaled and instantly relaxed when I saw it was indeed empty.

I hurried into the elevator and simultaneously jabbed the 'close door' button and the button for my floor with intense ferocity. The doors slid closed, and I was able to relax fully, knowing I was home free. Even if the elevator stopped to let other passengers on before reaching my floor, it would be fine. I was just another tenant on the way to my apartment, and there was nothing wrong or incriminating about that. The elevator made no stops on the way though, and several seconds later I was walking as quickly as I could while still looking nonchalantly toward my apartment.

I paused at the door before entering, thinking about the best way to go about having a conversation with Baz about pumping the brakes on all the killing I'd been doing. I mean, sure he'd been keeping his end of the deal, but the thing that worried me most was how easy it was for me to do it. I was actually enjoying myself, and I wasn't sure if that was what I was going for. Just then I remembered again how Baz said we were connected and wondered if he was already picking up on my concerns. I pushed open the door to find Baz standing on the counter, smoking as usual. The twisted smile on his warped little face told me everything I needed to know.

Mandiba followed closely and cautiously as Mephistopheles led him back past the pits and into the black mist that obscured the landscape. He hadn't shown his concern or fear over Mephistopheles telling him how he'd already seen the situation and how it 'plays out', but it was eating away at his insides. He wanted to believe the banished one was bluffing and trying to talk a big game in order to disarm Mandiba so as to manipulate him easier. A feat like that wasn't going to be easy though, since Mandiba's will was strong. Probably stronger then any being Mephistopheles had used his power on in the past, and he wondered if the human-lover was aware of the great strength he possessed.

"Where is it you're taking me to?" asked Mandiba.

Mephistopheles stopped and turned to face the hunter before answering.

"I understand your mistrust of me, and I know you have good reason to feel this way," he said. "But, it is you who has come to me for help, and in order for that to happen you will have to put those feelings aside. Like it or not, friend, we are a team now, albeit an unlikely one, but a team nonetheless."

The ancient creature stared into Mandiba's eyes as if he could read everything going on inside his head while he waited for a response.

"Fine then, demon," answered Mandiba. "I will put my trust in you if you can indeed help like you say you can, but if you cross me I will destroy you. Puppet of the Old Ones or not, I have been given the power and ability to do so. There will be no discussion."

"That's the spirit," said Mephistopheles, smiling mischievously. "Now, on with it."

He didn't react or acknowledge Mandiba's threat, which unsettled him even further. Mandiba said what he said because he believed it to be true, but was it possible Mephistopheles knew something he didn't? There was no way of knowing, so he resigned himself to his present situation with no other choice but to wait for the other shoe to drop if it indeed did. The thick, black mist cleared as they continued, revealing a towering black mountain not visible from the pits behind them. Mandiba thought he knew of every mountain range there was in Okanisis, but this one he had never seen. It towered higher than any of the others, and its peak disappeared into the gray clouds climbing higher into the red sky than he could see.

There was something else different about this mountain that set it apart from all the others. It was shiny and smooth like glass or some kind of precious stone, and as far as he could tell this wasn't the only aspect of this mountain that would make it difficult to climb. There didn't appear to be any crags or outcroppings to act as footholds. The entire mountain was smooth, shiny, and enormous.

"Don't worry, my friend," said Mephistopheles, "we're not climbing. Even I know what a fool's errand that would be."

"What is this? What are we doing here then?"

Mephistopheles answered by pointing to a small cave off to the left Mandiba hadn't noticed until just then. Shimmering gold light pulsed and radiated from the opening, and although it closely mimicked a flickering fire, Mandiba knew it was from something else.

"Please," said Mephistopheles, still pointing, "after you."

"Actually," said Mandiba, "why don't you go first."

"You checked your phone, right?" asked Baz for the fourth time.

"Yes," I said, monotone, "and yes I checked it the last time you asked, and the times before that as well."

He was referring to the bevy of constant texts I was getting from Elizabeth, each containing a picture racier than the one preceding it. This most recent one was an up-skirt shot she'd taken while sitting in one of the funeral parlor pews. She wanted to make it very clear to me that she wasn't wearing panties, and the message was coming through loud and clear. I had also just gotten off the phone with Nancy from work who, first off, wanted me to know she was in charge of calling everyone in the office to update them.

Her sad, mournful tone was put-on and affected by her begrudging attitude toward her assignment. She told me the official update was the police found no clues from watching the tape, and in fact were now leaning toward the possibility that the whole thing was an accident. She said, as far as they could see, it appeared Mr. Johansson lost his balance and fell just right to sustain the kind of injuries he had.

"Like a one in a million shot," she said into the receiver; the words dripped with her southern accent and false sympathy as they bounced around my brain.

One in a million shot? Shit, if she only knew. I don't remember hanging up with Nancy or if I had simply hung up on her, but I know that was when the picture-texts started.

"You check your phone?" asked Baz again, grinning with his trademark cigarette stuck confidently in the corner of his mouth.

I glanced absently at the screen to see an extreme, Georgia O'Keefe-style close up of Elizabeth's genitals. Either that or it was a pile of lunchmeat. The lighting in the shot wasn't the best but, regardless, it still made me horny.

"Yeah, right, I get it, and this is awesome," I said "but tell me again why I can't take a day or two off from killing people? I'm not morally opposed to it or anything like that, but it's just . . . exhausting."

I meant what I said too. Strangely enough I was feeling little to no remorse for the people I had already killed, but it was nerve-racking work. I just wanted to unwind for a day or two and take some time to enjoy the fruits of my labor. That wasn't in the cards, however, as Baz explained it to me thusly:

"Think about it like this," he said. "This entire new life that you've used me to help you create runs on batteries. If those batteries aren't kept constantly charged the whole thing is going to slow down and fall apart. You understand?"

"Uh, sure."

And I did understand. I understood what he was saying to me, but I didn't understand why the whole thing worked the way he was saying it did. I thought we were trading off one for one, tit-for-tat, a kill for a prize. Now he was saying to maintain the things he'd already given to me, I was going to have to provide him with a constant source of energy. How would I ever be able to enjoy any part of this 'new life' if I had to focus on killing people all the time to keep it from going away? It wasn't the most ideal situation for me, but Baz was quite insistent and persuasive as he often was. He told me eventually we would find a balance and things would become easier to manage, but right now everything was moving too fast to be balanced. Right now was not the time to slow things down.

I patted my pockets absently, searching for my smokes, when Baz, clearly sensing my need, produced one of his from the air and handed it to me. The tip blazed to life as I stuck the filter to my lips and pulled the strange smoke into my lungs. This shit was seriously starting to get heavy.

"Hey," said Baz. "You check your phone?"

I exhaled smoke and brought the tiny screen once again to my eye-level to see what part of her anatomy Elizabeth was showing off to me now, but this picture contained no nudity. It was a picture of an apartment door with the number prominently displayed at its center. It was my door, and my apartment number. I walked to the door, holding the phone, with the cigarette dangling from my mouth. I opened it to find a completely naked Elizabeth standing in the hallway with no regard for modesty. Suddenly keeping the batteries of this new life charged didn't seem like such a bad thing.

The sex was amazing, and my dick was raw and throbbing now as I sat on the stool I'd pulled up to my kitchen counter. I originally planned to leave the room naked to meet Baz, but decided against it, throwing my boxers on at the last second. I figured since Baz and I were connected I wouldn't have to worry about being naked around him, but I didn't want to add the additional layer of comfort to our relationship just yet. There was a turkey and Swiss sandwich on a plate in front of me, and as I anticipated its impending ingestion, I suddenly realized how hungry I was at the mere sight of it. Next to it was a stack of papers neatly stapled in the corner with the rather off-putting title 'Kill Schedule' emblazoned on the top line. Baz stood off to the side of the document, smoking and tapping his foot. The look on his face was a perfunctory smugness almost too perfect to not have been practiced.

"That Liz is a minx in the sack, huh?" he half asked and half declared. "What a lucky boy you are."

I tried to downplay the discomfort his statement made me feel, masking my chagrin by taking an overly large bite of the sandwich while pretending to read the stack of papers. I wouldn't allow myself to focus on any one section, but from my scan I could see it was incredibly detailed and included dates with times down to the minute and even seconds. I swallowed the bite of sandwich and placed the stapled stack of paper down next to the plate where I found it.

"Jesus, Baz," I said. "This is . . . really—"

"Detailed and specific, I know," he interrupted, "but it really lays it all out. I find an outline like this takes the guesswork out of things, and really makes it easier to wrap your head around."

"Easier?" I was flipping through the stack again and could have sworn it had gotten thicker over the last few seconds. "There's nothing easy about any of this. According to this you've got me killing someone every day, sometimes two in a day. How am I going to be able to pull this off while maintaining a new relationship, and new responsibilities at work, and . . . life?"

"Well, it's a good thing you have me to help take care of all those things for you. As long as you stick to the 'Kill Schedule' you won't have to worry about any of the work that goes into those things, but will still experience all the benefits such as an abundance of disposable income, and an abundance of dick-chafing sex."

"So my life would just be comprised of money, sex, and death?"

I had to admit to myself after saying it out loud, it didn't sound like such a bad thing. I mean, I would be getting what I wanted *all* the time, and wasn't that why I summoned Baz in the first place?

"That's right," said Baz, his response pulling me from the track my train of thought was heading down. "Stick with me, and the two of us will go far."

There was something off-putting about the way Baz said *the two of us* that made me feel like he was getting more than just 'street cred' out of our relationship. I decided now wasn't the time to press this issue though.

"Look, man," I started, "this is great, I really mean it, but this is a lot of work. Like, a whole lot, and I don't mean to not sound grateful for everything you've done for me so far but there's got to be a better way. Right?"

I cringed inwardly at my use of an old *As Seen on T.V.* infomercial catchphrase, but I was serious. There had to be a different approach to all of this that would make it easier on me and Baz. Maybe it was just my old *work smarter not harder* mentality that was screaming from within to be heard, but I honestly wasn't even sure that mode of thought could be applied to a situation like this.

"A better way," said Baz, putting his chubby hands behind his back as he began to pace the counter in front of me, the sandwich, and the 'Kill Schedule'. "Funny that you mention that, because there is."

"There is? Well, what is it?"

"Slow down, chum," Baz replied. "There is indeed a *better* way, but I'm not sure how easy it's going to be for you."

The gold poop medallion grew warm against my bare chest, and it might have been my eyes playing tricks on me, but I swore it started radiating a faint, gold light.

Mephistopheles smiled and was compliant with Mandiba's request for him to enter the cave first. He ducked, stepped into the stone mouth without hesitation, and led Mandiba toward the source of gold light. He kept his hands behind his back, one held within the other without looking back as he led the way. They hadn't gone more than thirty feet or so through the narrow, claustrophobic tunnel before a huge inner cavern opened up, revealing the light source and their destination. The cavern's dome-shaped ceiling was easily over fifty feet high at its highest point, striking a dizzying contrast to the cramped space they'd just walked through. However, what truly drew Mandiba's eyes upward wasn't the ceiling, but what was hanging from it. Dangling from the center of the ceiling's curved apex by its hind legs was an albino, bat-like creature that hung more than halfway to the floor. A hideous, fang-filled snarl writhed its way across the thing's face.

Mandiba flinched, not sure if he were more taken aback by the size of the bat or how dazzlingly white it was. It was the absence of all color in a way he'd never seen before. His eyes went down the long body of the bat-thing and continued past its head to the ground below where the gold light was radiating up at him. The light was its brightest at this point and Mandiba had to squint until his eyes adjusted to see the light's source. It was shit. It was a pile of golden, glowing bat shit piled up at least two feet above his head. Mandiba stepped back and assumed a combative stance.

"What is the meaning of this, demon?" he shouted. "What kind of trick are you trying to pull on me?"

Mephistopheles turned around slowly on his heels to face Mandiba and kept his hands behind his back.

"This is not a trick, my friend." The words flowed from him in waves of cool confidence. "This . . . is what you came to me for."

24

I couldn't bring myself to think about what Baz told me the *better way* would be and pushed it from my mind by focusing on my task at hand—my first stop on the 'Kill Schedule'. It turned out the Schedule wasn't really a linear-style document. There were several indexes and appendices to reference for each scheduled kill that told me what part of my life it was creating, enhancing, maintaining, or manipulating. It was all quite confusing, and I couldn't bring myself to trust Baz completely with this, but for now I didn't have a choice.

I decided to follow the Schedule in order to buy some time so I could think. I didn't know what about, but I needed to reflect, if nothing else. Not now though, or at least not at this exact second. Right now at this exact second I was supposed to jam the screwdriver I was holding into Mr. Tinson from 4B's eye as soon as he answered his door. Now, I know that sounds like I would never get away with it, but according to appendix 2.c.12f there's a kill I will do in three days that erases this, and four additional upcoming kills between now and then. By 'erase' I don't mean like they never happened, but in the sense that my involvement will have been erased. Now I just needed this jerkoff to answer his door so I could get on with my life.

The giant bat creature snarled, growled, and drooled as it squeezed more golden guano from its ass, which was up toward the ceiling of the cave. The stuff dripped out in a few steamy spurts and landed on the pile with a wet slap and sizzled as it cooled and hardened in seconds. Mephistopheles walked to the pile, pulled away a gold chunk, and approached Mandiba with his arm extended for him to examine it. Mandiba looked but did not take it from his hand. To him, it looked exactly like a piece of excrement would after being dipped in gold, only this wasn't dipped. It was solid gold all the way through. Mandiba could do nothing but silently stare at the thing until Mephistopheles finally spoke.

"By the look on your face I would guess you have no idea what this is."

Mandiba shook his head.

"This," continued Mephistopheles, "is what is causing you such headaches in your searching. *This* is how the renegade you seek made his escape, and *this* is also the reason you can't see where he is."

"Okay," said Mandiba finally, "it looks like golden bat shit, but I'm sure you're going to tell me that it's so much more, right?"

"Yes and no," Mephistopheles said, tossing the gold chunk over his shoulder where it bounced off the rest of the pile and landed a few feet away from it. "It is just golden bat shit, that much is true, but you're also right about there being more to it. For ages the golden guano was the only key to unlocking the door between our realm and others like Earth."

"I thought that was a power only the Old Ones held dominion over to temporarily grant to those they deemed fit?"

"It is now. Eons ago when the Old Ones finally honed their great power, and were able to regulate the passage between realms they knew they had to eliminate the golden guano in order to have complete and total control. That's why our big, white friend is here with me in the pits, which seems to be the rug the Old Ones sweep their problems under."

Mephistopheles turned to admire the white bat with a look of admiration. A commiseration of sorts passed between the demon and the beast with an intangible understanding the two shared for their present plight.

"Why banish the creature?" asked Mandiba. "Why wouldn't the Old Ones just destroy it to keep something like this from happening?"

"As fond of destruction as the Old Ones are, they aren't much on destroying their own kind. As far as I go, well, I'm not sure why they spared me, but I'm starting to wonder if death would be a welcome alternative to my banishment."

"Are you saying that this thing is . . .?"

"One of the Old Ones, yes," interrupted Mephistopheles. "Her name is Samnisa, and she was born from the same conversion of energy and cataclysm as Them. When the others found they could not control her great power they bound her in a state of hibernation, or suspended animation if you will, and hid her away out here. Poor thing is locked away somewhere in her mind unable to escape, but they couldn't stop her from producing the very thing they banished her here for. They just hope no one will ever find her, or it."

"But someone did," said Mandiba. "Someone got ahold of this stuff, and is doing exactly what the Old Ones feared, but how would anyone know unless they had access to information only They knew? You don't think it could be . . . one of Them do you?"

"Bravo, my friend," said Mephistopheles with a hint of sarcasm.

"Now that you've put it all together, what do you propose we do?"

Mandiba stepped back and looked at the great white bat once again. Her eyes, while open, were glossed over and distant. Drool slowly leaked from the sides of her mouth and formed slimy pools in the crevices and crannies of the golden shit pile below. Still, he thought he detected a vague awareness in the creature, or maybe he convinced himself of it because he so badly wanted it to be there.

The thought that one of the Old Ones would ever try to break off from the others in an attempt to seize sole control over Okanisis was something Mandiba had never considered, but now that he was it didn't seem like a farfetched thing to think. What bothered Mandiba most was, if this were the case, why hadn't he picked up on it? He considered himself to be perceptive to the degree of seeing through any façade. He knew the Old Ones were powerful, but he wondered if it were he who was not as powerful as They had let him believe.

"Do you know how to . . . use this? Make it work?" Mandiba pointed at the shimmering shit pile as he asked the banished one.

"Why do you ask questions you already know the answer to?" he replied.

"Well . . . why are you still here then?"

"I'm sorry, Mandiba," Mephistopheles softened as he spoke. "Allow me to explain the predicament of my punishment. Back before I crossed over I'd heard whispered tales and legends about Samnisa, and the power her golden gift could bestow upon he who possessed it. I knew finding her would be the only way I would ever be able to leave this realm, so I started chasing down every bit of information on her throughout Okanisis. I took every story into consideration no matter how ridiculous or contradictory, and eventually I pieced together a map that led me to this very place."

"Yes, and then you used this shit to make your escape," snapped Mandiba. "I know your story, demon! Why can't you do it again?"

"If you did indeed *know* my story," quipped Mephistopheles, "then you would know why I can't do it again. The Old Ones made it so I couldn't use the golden guano to travel to the realm I loved so dearly by taking my soul."

"What?"

"To ensure my punishment would stick They removed my soul

from my body and did who knows what with it, but it can't be as bad as being banished to these pits. So, in short, since I no longer have a soul, I'm unable to harness the power."

"What does that mean?" asked Mandiba, losing his patience. "Are you saying this won't work to help me find the escaped one?"

"Oh no, my friend," he answered. "Now that you're here we can get it to work just fine."

I stayed in my apartment all day after stabbing Mr. Tinson in the eye with a screwdriver. I jammed it in his right eye as soon as he opened the door, not giving him a moment to react or process that he was in danger. He was surprised, to say the least, and I used my forward momentum to push him back into his apartment. I caught the door with the side of my foot and shut it behind me as we both stepped in. He was screaming a bit more than I had hoped, but when I rammed the butt of the screwdriver with the palm of my hand it sunk three more inches into his head, and he collapsed at my feet, silent and dead. I wiped the sticky, warm sluice expelled from his burst eyeball off my chin with the back of my hand, turned around, counted to three, and walked out quickly, closing the door behind me.

I was too impatient to wait for an elevator so I took the stairs, not concerned if anyone saw me or not. Being seen using the stairs wasn't going to be something that would instantly implicate me in this particular crime, and even if it did I was sure I was scheduled to kill someone in the next day or so that would change it all anyway. When I got back to the apartment I sat on the sofa, watching episodes of *Diff'rent Strokes* with Baz chain-smoking in silence. Every time my cigarette was about to reach the filter Baz would tap my arm and present me with a freshly lit replacement.

Of course there was no work again today in observation of Mr. Johansson's death and because the place was still sort of a gruesome crime scene. Elizabeth had left early in the morning to handle more of what she said were the 'boring and stupid' details of her dead husband's funeral and estate. After that she was supposed to go by her place to grab a bunch of things she wanted to bring over, like her hairdryer and other girl-type shit. This was just as well because I needed some time to just brood over things. Mainly what Baz and I had talked about that morning a few hours before dawn.

It was raining and had been all day. The sky was the type of dark that made it hard to tell what time of day it was, which was fine with me since that was exactly how I felt inside. Dark, gray, and unsure. What only days ago seemed like an easy and fun new bartering system had quickly turned into a scheduled quota of bloodbaths I was required to meet from now until the end of time. That is unless . . .

Baz tapped my arm, breaking me from my unproductive train of thought, and presented me with a fresh cigarette I wasn't even aware I was ready for. I removed the one from my mouth, stamped it out in an ashtray on the armrest, and put the new one between my severely chapped lips.

"Check your phone," said Baz, not looking away from the television, as if terrified he might miss one of Gary Coleman's famous 'what you talkin' about, Willis?' lines.

I do, and find a text from Liz saying she's on her way over from her place and she had several 'surprises' for me. The text was, of course, accompanied by a picture of her licking one of her own nipples. I couldn't tell which one it was but it was moot since I knew she could do both. I pushed myself off the couch and started shuffling toward the bathroom, trying to shake the pins and needles from my sleeping legs and feet.

"Where you goin'?" asked Baz, still not breaking eye contact with Mr. Drummond.

"To take a shit," I said without breaking stride.

"Good idea," he answered. "You should get it out now before Liz fucks it out of you later."

I shut and locked the bathroom door behind me and sat on the toilet but I didn't really have to shit. I just needed to think by myself for a minute, so I sat there with my eyes closed, absently clutching the gold poop medallion in my left hand. I couldn't remember if I'd taken it off at all since Baz had given it to me, and I was starting to wonder if that was the best decision on my part. This thing was protecting me, sure, but only because it *seemed* to benefit me in some form or another and kept me from getting caught. I mean, it was a magical object from another plane of existence and just because it literally looked like shit didn't make it any less powerful and creepy.

I let go of the thing, letting it swing from the chain around my neck and bounce lightly against my bare chest a few times. I was only wearing boxer shorts since I'd taken off my bloody, eyeball-pus covered clothes as soon as I'd gotten in. Baz told me just to ball them up and throw them in the corner. He said he'd take care of it. That wasn't the only thing Baz said he'd 'take care of' on my mind. I tried again not to think about the conversation we had in the day's early hours, but I *had* to think about it. I mean, I had to at least consider it, didn't I? I guess the main drawback was the fear, but I was sure Baz could just wave his hand, so to speak, and make that go away too.

It was my soul. That's what Baz said was the 'better way' to solve both of our problems. He told me I could trade my soul in lieu of having to kill people to keep my whole 'dream life' charged up and on track. He said I could have anything I wanted while I was alive, not have to kill, and he would have all the power and clout in his home world he wanted. The only drawback was, after my body died, my soul would most likely be an eternal slave to some old gods back in his realm. He tried to sugarcoat it by telling me these gods of his would more than likely get tired of me after a millennium or two and release me. Then, my soul could wander through wherever he said he was from for the rest of time.

I closed my eyes and massaged my temples, trying to wrap my head around millennia of slaving followed by endless wandering through another dimension, but the thought made my brain ache. On the other hand, the promise of unlimited luxury and wishes while alive was hard to turn down despite the price. I could also continue following Baz's schedule for daily killing, which was a ton of work but doable if I stayed sharp. My only qualm was the amount of variables that went in to maintaining the Schedule and what would happen if I fucked something up. What if I got caught in traffic and missed my kill for the day because they got on a train to another city before I could get to them? What if I was sick and couldn't function enough to get to the bathroom, let alone muster enough energy to kill someone.

When I thought about these things it occurred to me the Schedule was more than likely designed to set me up for failure, thereby making the single soul sacrifice sound that much more appealing. Everything was going fine now, sure, but it had only been a few days and, between the fucking and the killing, I was exhausted. I heard the front door of my apartment open and Liz call out for me in a low, sultry tone that told my brain sex was on the way. I needed to talk to Baz about this whole 'soul' thing and badly, but it could wait. Right now the tent I'd pitched in my boxers became my main priority.

27

Mandiba couldn't believe how careless he'd been. How could he let his guard down and have this happen to him, the great and powerful seeker? Mandiba the hunter, they'd called him at one time, but now he would surely forever be known as Mandiba the fool. He struggled, but could barely move due to the tightness of what was restraining him. He couldn't see even though his eyes were indeed open, but he didn't need sight to know where he was. He was in the belly of Samnisa, the giant white bat.

Mandiba was right about his hunch that one of the Old Ones was double-crossing him, it just turned out to be an Old One he didn't know existed until a few minutes ago. It happened so fast, he debated whether or not he could have abated the attack even if he was on high alert. Mandiba could feel something happening to him, and he knew it wasn't good but he wasn't exactly sure what it was. He was wrapped so tightly in the slippery lining of the bat's stomach it was hard for him to feel anything except a dull burning all over. He tried to struggle again but it was no use, and even if he weren't being held so tightly he would never be able to get enough purchase against the slick lining to push his way out.

It turned out Mephistopheles had only told him half the truth about himself and Samnisa. It was true the Old Ones placed the giant bat into a magic-induced stasis when they banished her to the pits, and it was true they had stripped Mephistopheles of his soul as well. While this took away his ability to manipulate the magic of the golden shit, it didn't take away his ability to manipulate magic in general. Because of this oversight, Mephistopheles manipulated the magic keeping Samnisa in hibernation to basically control her like his puppet, and that was how Mandiba ended up inside of her. One second they were discussing the loss of Mephistopheles' soul, and the next the bat had struck from its perch, snatched Mandiba in her mouth, and swallowed him down whole.

Suddenly the taut, slick lining holding Mandiba in place began to vibrate gently before turning terribly turbulent. Mandiba wasn't aware he was also upside down in the bat's stomach until a hole opened, letting in the light. It was Samnisa's open mouth, and the next thing he knew Mandiba was spun around and rushing head-first toward the ground as he was ejected from the Old One's stomach. A torrent of yellow bile followed behind and covered Mandiba a second after he'd landed. He struggled to get to his feet and wipe the slime from his eyes, hoping to not be taken by surprise again.

"Where are you, demon!" he howled. "What is the meaning of this?"

Mandiba's eyes cleared and he could see Mephistopheles was standing exactly where he had been before the bat swallowed him, but now he was looking up. Mandiba followed his eye line to see what he was looking at. There was something being expelled by Samnisa but it wasn't gold guano, it was a pink and purple orb that crackled and popped with energy as it floated gently down to land in the palm of Mephistopheles' hand. He held the orb up to his eyes for a moment to inspect it, then pressed it to his chest until he'd absorbed it.

Mandiba felt an emptiness ringing throughout him and knew what had happened. Mephistopheles had taken his soul. He'd used the sleeping Old One to somehow extract it, then he'd taken it for himself so he could use the power of Samnisa's gift. Mandiba dropped to his knees, partially from sudden exhaustion and partially from the disgust he felt for himself. Mephistopheles took a deep breath, smiled, and approached the kneeling seeker.

"Well, I see you have this all figured out then," he said. "No need for me to indulge you in lengthy, theatrical explanations. I thank you for your soul, and for taking my place."

"Taking . . . your place?"

Mandiba could hardly muster the words as energy flowed out of him like water through a drain.

"Yes, my new friend," Mephistopheles answered slyly. "I'm leaving now, and you will serve the rest of my eternal sentence in the pits. I do appreciate it, by the way."

"Eternal . . . pits . . ."

That was all Mandiba could manage as the last of his strength and power left him. His head hit the floor and, as everything went black, he hoped the light would never return.

Baz seemed anxious and was visibly agitated as I strolled into the kitchen for our late night chat. I was wearing only my boxers and the medallion, and I rubbed my crotch to situate my sore and thoroughly throttled cock as I sat on a stool at the counter.

"About goddamn time, lover boy," Baz spat between the chimneystacks' worth of smoke he was spewing. "I'm surprised you're not just a dried out husk at this point with all the sucking that bitch does!"

I straightened instantly as my face went flush with rage over what he said about Liz. Baz saw the flash of anger in my eyes and met it with one of his own, momentarily locking us in a pissing match of a staring contest. Baz softened first, flashing a tight smile and shrugging in concession.

"Okay, hey," he started, "sorry about that. Clearly I crossed a line, but all things considered, it's still not a bad deal, am I right?"

I had no other choice but to accept Baz's backhanded apology since he was right, and I wasn't clever enough to come up with a witty retort anyway. He produced a cigarette from the air above his head, and it lit itself as he passed it to me. I accepted the makeshift peace offering and took a long slow pull from it, allowing the smoke to exit my lungs slowly through my nostrils.

"So, what's got your . . . panties in a wad?" I asked, cursing myself for not being able to think of something actually clever to say.

I put my elbows on the counter and rested my head in my left hand while holding the cigarette in the other. To my right sat only the 'Kill Schedule' with no accompanying sandwich this time. The stack of paper was creased and worn from my incessant flipping through to check the index and appendices, but I couldn't help but think it looked thicker than it had only hours ago. Baz saw me give the stack a double take.

"I know what you're thinking," he started, "and you're right. Some addendums and additions had to be made to the Schedule."

I glanced back down at the stack of paper to gesture to it with my non-cigarette hand, and it looked like it had gotten even thicker over the last few seconds.

"Some? This thing is starting to look like the goddamn Yellow Pages. What gives?"

"The Schedule is what we call a *living document*, which, as you know, means it's in a constant state of . . . change, as it must respond and adapt to what's happening around it. Also, this document is really alive."

I glanced back down at the Schedule and swore I heard a soft, low growl. I wanted to push it across the counter, but was afraid I might lose a finger to the thing.

"What does that mean? Is this *thing* just going to keep getting bigger and bigger until there aren't enough hours in the day or people in existence for me to keep up?"

I was trying to keep my rise in emotion from causing the volume of my voice to rise with it. I didn't want to wake Elizabeth and have to explain any of this. Besides, she'd probably demand more sex from me and my dick had had all it could take for the time being.

"Maybe not," said Baz, pausing to take a quick cigarette puff, "but probably so. It just really all depends."

The creature was curt in a way that made me feel like he thought he had one over on me. I hoped I was wrong, because I didn't like what the thought of me being right would mean.

"Depends?!"

I raised my voice, this time not caring if I woke up Elizabeth or the neighbors. I set my hands palms down on the counter in front of me, pulled my face close to Baz's, and pulled the volume of my voice back to a controlled smooth whisper.

"And what might this *depend* on?"

Baz smiled at my attempt at intimidation, letting me know without a doubt he was calling my bluff. What was I going to do anyway? I'm no tough guy. Baz smoked and casually strolled down the counter a foot or so before turning back around toward me.

"It depends on a lot of things. You know, there are just so many variables that make things so . . . unpredictable. Basically, there are quite a number of variables you have no control over, and *those* variables affect the Schedule. You can think of it as a butterfly effect of sorts if that helps you to fully understand."

"What the hell does an Ashton Kutcher movie have to do with any of this?"

I didn't yell that time, but I did speak a tad louder than an expectable inside voice should be.

"Sweetie?"

I froze when I heard the hushed, breathy whisper behind me. It was Elizabeth.

"Are you . . . are you talking to someone out here?"

Shit. I had woken Elizabeth, and I tried to get my growing rage in check before turning around to greet her. My mind was a clusterfuck of scattered thoughts at the moment, and I scrambled to think of what to tell her. I flashed Baz a pleading look before I turned from the counter, not knowing what I even expected him to do.

"Hey, my dear," I said softly as I faced her.

Elizabeth was just inside the bedroom, leaning luridly against the doorframe while absently twirling a tendril of soft brown hair around her finger. The light from the bedroom behind outlined her petite, sexy figure and highlighted the smooth curves of her body. She was naked save for one of my V-neck undershirts, which came down just past the lower curve of her butt cheeks. I didn't have to guess she wasn't wearing panties underneath, and neither did my dick as it attempted to draw blood into it despite the soreness from our earlier sexual romp. Just seeing this partial silhouette of the dream girl I'd only days ago thought was impossible to obtain was enough to make me kill anyone anywhere.

"I'm sorry I woke you up," I continued. "I was just . . . going over some documents for work."

I gestured to the conveniently placed thick stack of paper on the counter behind me as if I needed to prove my reason for being awake. Elizabeth didn't respond, hovering motionless in the doorway, looking stiff and statuesque. Her soft curves became a bit harder and more angular like she'd all of a sudden tensed up every muscle in her body at once.

"I'll just be a few more minutes," I said, "and then I'll be right back in there with you, I promise."

Again, Elizabeth answered me with silence, but it wasn't just her; I was surrounded by silence. I don't mean that it was just really quiet either. This was an odd silent stillness that made my skin crawl. I couldn't hear the soft hum of conditioned air blowing through the apartment, or the low rumble of the refrigerator, or any cars passing by outside. For a second I thought I was having a stroke or a brain embolism or something and this was some drawn out, extended version of my last moment before I dropped over dead. Baz cleared his throat from the counter behind me, and the noise was deafening in comparison to the vacuum-like silence I was experiencing. I whirled around to face the impish, chain-smoking creature.

"She can't hear you right now, my friend," he said.

"Why? What's going on? Why does everything seem so weird?"

I felt lightheaded and plopped back down onto the stool, gripping the counter with both hands.

"I wanted to buy us a little time so we could finish our discussion," he said, "so I stopped time."

"Stopped time?"

"Yeah, sorry about not giving you any warning. I understand it can make your kind feel pretty shitty until your body adapts."

I held onto the edge of the counter, barely able to process what Baz said due to my head suddenly beginning to spin so fast I thought my brains were scrambling. Nausea worked its way in from my fingers and toes until reaching my stomach, pushing it up into my throat. I thought my stomach and other vital organs were about to be ejected from my mouth when all of a sudden all the unpleasantness stopped and everything in my body began to feel normal again.

"You'll be fine in a couple minutes," continued Baz, and he was right.

I all at once felt great and held my two fingers out to Baz, signaling him to give me a cigarette, which he pulled from the air and placed already lit between those same two fingers. I sucked greedily on the thing, letting the smoke calm my mind and put me at baseline again. I wanted to look back over my shoulder at the frozen Liz, but I was afraid the sight would disorient me again, so I took another drag and stared down Baz.

"So you can stop time?" I asked. "How many kills do I need to make to cover this trick?"

"Yeah, I can stop time, but only for short periods so we gotta talk fast, and don't worry about it. This one's on me."

"How convenient," I muttered, dragging hard on the cigarette again.

"Have you thought about what we talked about?"

"I've actually tried to do everything I could not to."

There was another grumbling from the Schedule by my elbow, and I watched it shuffle and twitch while it grew in length by several more pages.

"I understand it might not seem ideal, but it's really an opportunity you should count yourself lucky to even have presented to you."

"The loss of my soul and eternal slavery in some pseudo-hell-type realm sounds like a really great opportunity," I said, smashing my cigarette out on the counter, not wanting to reach across the Schedule to grab an ashtray despite the fact the document sounded like it was snoring.

"Enough with this shit," snapped Baz, clearly put off by my sarcasm. His black orb eyes began to glow red around the rims. "Time is running out for you and me! If you don't want to give up your soul, fine. You'll just have to keep killing and killing while the Schedule gets longer and longer until you can't keep up, and everything in your life will go to absolute shit. You'll die alone, penniless, and probably in prison, and then your precious soul will float off into any number of realms where you'll more than likely end up a slave for all eternity anyway. This way, you know what you're getting into, and you get something out of it. Sounds like a no-brainer to me, but I've never understood why you humans process thoughts the way you do."

Shit. When he said it like that it made total sense. It was a *no-brainer* and an *opportunity* I would be out of my mind not to take. Baz was right, and with the uncertainty of what would happen to me when I die anyway, I owed it to myself to indulge my gluttonous greedy side to the fullest extent until the end of my life. Besides, I'm sure Baz's magic could help keep me in excellent health far longer than the average person who didn't have access to such a thing. There was only one thing Baz said that still gave me pause.

"What did you mean when you said time is running out for you too?" I asked. "I understand I'd be at the mercy of the growing Schedule, but how does any of this affect you?"

"I told you, it helps me out in my own realm in a way you wouldn't really understand. Just trust me when I say we have a finite window of time to go the soul route before you're fucked by the Schedule and I'm fucked . . . out of what I want."

"What you want? How about you put it into laymen's terms for me?"

"I'll have to go back, okay! I'm not supposed to be here, and I'll be forced to go back. That is something I DO NOT want to do, so you see, that is why time is of the essence."

Okay, so Baz was getting something out of our relationship that was far more than just 'street cred' and, while I figured as much, it sounded good to hear him say it. As the seconds ticked by they slowly melted away the apprehension I felt about trading off my soul bit by bit until I finally gave the very frustrated Baz the answer he wanted to hear.

"Fine then," I said, looking into his red-rimmed eyes, "I'll do it."

The red light dimmed instantly and an unsettling smile cracked its way across Baz's face.

"You're making a very smart decision," he said, soft and low. "You won't regret it."

"Sure," I quipped, "so what do we need to do? Do I just sign a piece of paper, or do we light a candle and do some chanting?"

"Just meet me here in the kitchen at the same time tomorrow, and we'll perform the ceremony."

"Wait, tomorrow?" I asked, flipping through the Schedule without regard for the safety of my fingers. "This says I have to kill two people before then. Can't we just do it now?"

"Stick to the Schedule until tomorrow night, but right now you better get back in the bedroom, tiger."

There was a loud pop and cold rush of air telling me that Baz had un-stopped time. I gained my bearings much quicker than before and heard Elizabeth calling for me again from behind.

"Sweetheart, stop working and come to bed. I want you."

"Be right there, dear," I said, scanning the counter for Baz, who had vanished.

I got off the stool and headed for the bedroom while the golden poop medallion began getting warm against my chest.

I didn't sleep at all for the rest of that night despite the extra physical second round of sex after I went back to the bedroom. My body was exhausted, my dick was raw and throbbing, but my mind just wouldn't shut down. It was filled with terrifying thoughts fueled by ultra-high levels of anxiety mixed with excitement. I couldn't believe I was actually trading my soul for a lifetime of luxurious living that would allow me to have anything I desired on a whim. I chose not to dwell on the tradeoff and what it meant for me in the afterlife. There was nothing I could do to change it, after all, and I wanted to enjoy my wish-filled life without constantly thinking about the black cloud hanging over my head.

I got out of bed before Elizabeth was awake, took a shower, got dressed, and sat at the kitchen counter pretending to eat breakfast while I waited for her. I'd already decided I wasn't going to work again today even though I received an email the night before saying the office would be open today and there were going to be a couple grief counselors there if anyone needed to talk about what happened. Since today was the day of Elizabeth's husband's actual funeral I'd already sent an email saying I would be taking a personal day to attend the service. Elizabeth, however, had told me I didn't need to be there and nor did I want to. So as far as she knew I was going to work. I really just wanted another day to take everything in and process not only what had happened but what was going to happen.

Elizabeth emerged dressed in the requisite black, modest, funeral-type dress although she exuded a cheerfulness that contradicted her attire. She kissed me deeply as she said goodbye and gave my sore manhood a hearty squeeze, which revived the small amount of pain that had subsided.

"I've got to take care of wrapping everything up with this whole deal," she said, emphasizing the callousness in her tone with the words *this whole deal* referring to her husband's funeral. "Anyway, I'll be back after you're home from work since I need to sign a bunch of paperwork, and I'm going to stop by the old house for a few more things I want to bring over."

"Sounds good," I answered through a mouthful of Frosted Flakes as she walked out the door.

I hadn't seen Baz all morning but when the door shut, as if on cue, he stepped out from behind the toaster and strolled across the counter toward me, smoking and smiling.

"Playing hooky today, I see," he said while exhaling thick, yellowed smoke.

"Well, I kind of have a pretty full day," I replied. "The Schedule changed again in the last few hours, so now I have three kills I need to take care of, not to mention I'm selling my soul later tonight. I'd like to get all the unpleasantness out of the way early so I can have some time to myself to . . . reflect."

"About that . . ." Baz paused and materialized a cigarette for me. I figured he was trying to soften the blow of some bad news he was about to deliver, so I cringed and accepted said cigarette. "Our time table has been slightly changed."

"In what way?"

"We've got to do it sooner than tonight."

"That's fine with me," I said, feeling relieved of my current stress for exactly one second before an entirely different stress rushed in to take its place. "That means I don't have to go do these stupid kills."

I heard the Schedule growl at me from across the counter, but I ignored it. What I couldn't ignore was how nervous Baz seemed and how it affected his mannerisms and vocal cadence. It made me feel like something was wrong. Something so wrong Baz wanted to keep it from me.

"Why did the time table change?" I asked, hoping to get more out of him.

"It's really a lot to explain, at least more than we have time for at the moment. Just think about it like launching missiles from a submarine; you gotta have some other guy there so you can both turn keys at the same time, or it won't work."

"What does launching missiles from a submarine have to do with you taking my soul?"

"Because," Baz fumed impatiently, "it takes me and somebody else to turn our keys to make this happen, and right now that somebody else is very ready to turn his key so we have to too. Okay?!"

I stopped myself from making a sarcastic comment to further goad Baz into full-on rage. What did I care anyway whether I lost my soul now or tonight? I lost it either way.

"Good enough for me," I said, straightening up in the stool. "What do I need to do?"

The frustration seemed to melt away from Baz as he slowly strolled down the counter toward me. His red-rimmed eyes glowed brighter with each step, and I could feel the medallion growing warm against my chest.

"Don't worry about that," said a much calmer Baz. "Just sit tight, and I'll take care of everything."

Mephistopheles hovered four feet off the ground with legs crossed in front of him, his hands resting palm down on each knee, and his eyes closed. On the ground in front of him lay the soulless and incapacitated Mandiba while the semi-paralyzed giant white bat hung motionless just behind him. On the ground directly beneath Mephistopheles was a pentagram surrounded by foreign symbols unknown to most outside of the Old Ones and the slippery demon. The symbols glowed the same dull purple of Mandiba's soul when it was expelled by Samnisa.

Mephistopheles' eyes were closed but he could very much see, and what he was seeing was his opportunity to escape Okanisis once and for all was nearly in his grasp. It wouldn't be long before his co-conspirator had everything lined up to allow him to cross over, and this time it would be for good. Not even the Old Ones would be powerful enough to bring him back, and there would be nothing they could do about it. The pentagram glowed slightly brighter, and Mephistopheles clenched his hands into fists as the moment grew closer and closer.

Mandiba was completely numb and unable to move in any way and, in fact, wasn't even sure if he had a body anymore. Unlike

Mephistopheles' eyes, Mandiba's were open, and while he couldn't move he could see. He saw the smug face of his cohort-turned-enemy as he floated before him. He could see there was a purple glow coming from the ground below him, but he wasn't able to see what was causing it. Behind Mephistopheles hung the banished Old One whose power was manipulated to put Mandiba in the state he was in now.

Mandiba saw Mephistopheles' smile widen as the glow beneath him grew brighter and brighter, accompanied by a whirling rush of wind. The giant bat's face remained still, but Mandiba saw its eyes dilate from the intensity of the light. Mephistopheles' entire body began to glow now as it looked like he was being engulfed in purple flames. Then, just like that, he disappeared, and with him so did the purple glow. All Mandiba could see now was black again, not because he was unconscious, but because wherever Mephistopheles went he took the light there with him.

The last thing I remembered was talking to Baz about giving him my soul and him saying something about missiles and submarines. When I opened my eyes I found I couldn't move my legs and my arms felt like they were strapped to my sides by invisible rope. I was also floating a foot or so off the floor and was completely naked save for the golden poop medallion around my neck. It too seemed to be controlled by an invisible force as it floated up from the chain around my neck and hovered at eye-level. I was glad the thing wasn't touching my chest at the moment because it was glowing from the intense heat radiating from it.

A few feet in front of me was Baz, who was also hovering just above the shitty, makeshift altar I'd used to conjure him to me. Only now it was slightly modified. The blood and candles were gone, and the pentagram was surrounded by several strange symbols I didn't recognize from the small amount of research I'd done. The pentagram and the symbols gave off a pale, purple glow that made Baz look more sinister than I'd ever seen before. The soft, round, pseudo-facial features of the small blobby creature looked sharp and angular in the purple light, and his usual smile was replaced by a grimace cut in a straight line across. His eyes were shut, but the red glow still shone translucently through his eyelids.

As my awareness slowly returned I started struggling against my invisible bonds to no avail. I was completely incapacitated, unable to protect myself from anything that was about to happen. Baz's eyes suddenly shot open as if he could sense my attempts at moving; his formerly black eyes now glowed red. The hard lined snarl opened wide so he could speak to me, but his lips did not move and the voice that came out was not his.

"No point in struggling now," said the voice coming from Baz's mouth. "It's almost done."

I had no response, but even if I did I couldn't get my voice to work. It felt like a tiny hand was inside my neck strangling my vocal cords with enough pressure to keep them from vibrating even the tiniest bit. The purple light below Baz began to shine brighter, and I could feel the air turn cold around me. Baz's already open mouth began to stretch as he turned it up toward the ceiling, allowing it to open impossibly wide. The medallion, still floating at my eye level, began to rise higher until the chain slipped from around my neck and dangled from the golden shit medallion as it moved to the center of the room between Baz and I.

I started to feel a sensation in my chest like the medallion was somehow still burning me from across the room, and I realized it was. The burning spread across my body, pushing out from where it originated in my chest. It ran through my torso and down both legs all the way to my toes while doing the same down my arms and up my neck. I went from not being able to feel anything to the sensation of being burned alive in an instant, but I still couldn't move or scream. When the burning reached the edges of my body it changed course and made its way back to my chest where it collided into itself in a grand and intense explosion of pain. Then, I felt nothing once again.

A beam of purple light grew out of my chest where the pain explosion had occurred and slowly made its way through the air toward the floating medallion, crackling with electricity along the way. The light met the golden turd, causing its intense golden glow to turn purple. The medallion started to vibrate like it was about to explode when the same purple light shot from the other side of the turd and directly into Baz. The purple light began to rise from his open, upturned mouth but now there was something in the light. The higher it rose the more clearly I could see that *something* was actually a man wearing a white suit. The smile on his face seemed joyful, but the horns jutting from his forehead gave him a sinister quality.

The man continued to rise until his feet were exposed, and he stepped out from the gaping maw of Baz like he was stepping off the bus. That's when I remembered after this was all over I wasn't going to have to push anyone in front of a bus ever again, or down stairs, or off a roof. Once whatever was going on was over I would be soulless, but I would have the power to make my life everything I'd always wanted it to be. The horned, white-clad man smoothed the front of his jacket as the purple glow around him dimmed and then disappeared.

Baz's body hung in the air behind the man for just a moment, but instead of his mouth returning to normal his small, blob-ish body deflated and dropped to the ground. His formless husk re-minded me of an old rubber Halloween mask I'd had when I was a kid. I looked up from what was left of Baz to the man again as he approached the medallion, still glowing and floating in the air be-tween us. I realized something was very wrong. I wasn't sure what was supposed to happen in a ceremony like this, but I was pretty sure this one had gone off the rails.

"Actually, my friend," the man said as he plucked the medallion from the air, "you're half right."

What the hell? I knew I hadn't spoken because I tried again right then with the same results.

"I know it doesn't make sense," he said, continuing to approach me, holding up the golden poop, "but like I said earlier, it's almost over now and I thank you for your part in all of this. You've been instrumental in securing my freedom. Now, relax, because we've arrived at the end."

The medallion began to get closer, or so I thought, but it was actually I who was moving toward it, then into it. The brightness blinded me, and the ability to feel returned for a brief moment in the form of a warm rush, followed by a flash of cold, then nothing as I was swallowed by darkness.

Mephistopheles paced the living room, trying to calm his excitement as the reality of the situation began to fully set in. It had worked. He spent his centuries of banishment perfecting every detail, running every scenario, and devising solutions to every problem he could possibly run up against. Now here he was basking in the fruits of his effort in the form of escape. He noticed the spent and hollowed body of Baz at his feet, and kicked it into the corner with a pile of dirty clothes and candles that were never picked up after the first ceremony from days ago.

Mephistopheles didn't feel bad for tricking the poor creature. He was a weak, greedy, and gullible thing that wanted power he didn't have to work for. Mephistopheles lured Bazael to the pits years ago by projecting his aura just beyond the outskirts. He couldn't stray too far or the Old Ones would feel him and know what he was capable of. As long as he stayed in and around the pits the elder gods wouldn't know he was draining the power from one of their own they'd long since banished and forgotten. Baz wandered close enough to the pits one day for Mephistopheles to get into his mind and coax him closer. When he was fully in the pits Mephistopheles showed himself to Baz, and proposed Baz work for him in exchange for power he would receive from the giant bat.

Baz, not being particularly powerful, had no qualms with stealing it from the sleeping Old One. He was more than happy to help the banished demon for a shortcut to power. Thus, the plan began.

As detestable as Baz was to Mephistopheles, he possessed the exact qualities needed to make the plan work without a hitch. The small amount of power the greedy imp did possess was no match for Mephistopheles, and Baz was too stupid to even attempt to think of a way to double cross him. The subject needed to be from Earth and had to possess the same flawed characteristics as the imp, and Mephistopheles projected Baz's energy across the realms to find a perfect match. Once that was done and Baz was sent through, Mephistopheles had nothing left to do but sit back and wait for the dominos he'd so intricately arranged to fall. And fall they did.

He allowed the Old Ones to sense Baz's passing over to Earth, but did not allow them to see where the escape took place. The pits themselves gave off an energy Mephistopheles learned to manipulate and use against them to block the location of the portal from their nearly all-seeing eyes. He knew they would employ the services of their precious Mandiba, and he also knew after Mandiba was unable to track the portal down he would come straight to the pits like a lamb to the slaughter. The only surprising thing was it happened so quickly, but he had no problem with that. He figured Baz would have to string his Earthly foil along until Mandiba finally came knocking, but he showed up much sooner than Mephistopheles gave him credit for.

He walked over to the soulless, and now also lifeless, body of the Earth man who jumped at the chance to kill his way to a perfect life. Humans were a weak and flawed design since their bodies couldn't survive once the soul had departed. Mephistopheles released the body from the psychic bindings, and it flopped to the floor in a broken heap. Several bones snapped and pierced the skin, which caused a large puddle of blood to form beneath the former man. It was an inconvenience to have to dispose of the body, but there was plenty of time for that. Mephistopheles strolled to the window, threw open the curtain, and marveled at the world before him. A world he would never have to leave again. The click of the door snapped him from his daydream, and he turned to see Elizabeth walking into the apartment, her arms loaded with bags.

"Honey," she called, slamming the door behind her with her foot. "I'm . . . holy shit."

The scene was gruesome to say the least, and the second it took her to process what she was seeing was all Mephistopheles needed to get into her mind. She looked up from the bloody heap that had once been a man she'd only hours ago been making love to, met the demon's eyes, and smiled.

"Hello, my darling," she said, staring ahead blankly.

"Welcome home, my love," he answered.

It was a strange, alien feeling of floating detachment, but I'm not even sure if that's an accurate way to describe it. I don't think I could accurately use the word 'feeling' to describe anything at that point since I couldn't feel anything. I couldn't see anything either, and I really just thought I was dead. Any moment, I expected my last remaining flicker of consciousness to evaporate or dissolve back into the energy of the universe, and I would just be gone. That didn't happen though. Instead, I continued to pass through the thick, suffocating darkness for hours, or minutes, or maybe even seconds. I had no concept of time or anything else for that matter, and I remained in this state for a period of time I was unable to feel passing or even perceive existed.

Then, as suddenly as I had stopped feeling anything, I began to feel again. At first the sensation was jarring and brutal, but only because I had to learn what feeling was like again. After the initial shock I could feel a change in temperature all around me. First it was cool, then drastically colder, but only for a brief moment, as if I'd walked through an icy waterfall. The shocking cold turned warm in an instant, and the temperature around me continued to rise to an uncomfortable heat. I figured this was the sensation of death ripping me apart and hurling my pathetic ego and id back into the massive universal energy I was born from years ago.

The heat reached a crescendo, and I prepared for the end of an existence that didn't come. I felt the temperature begin to lower around me, although not half as fast as I would have liked. Familiar sensations began to creep back in as I became aware I had limbs again. I wiggled my fingers and toes as the feeling of their attachment came back to me, and the cloud of abstract thought began to dissipate from my mind. I allowed several moments to pass as the sensation of existing again ran up and down my body. I wasn't dead, that much I knew for sure, but something still didn't feel quite right. I thought maybe the shock of the experience I'd just been through was still lingering and making me feel uncomfortable in my own skin. I could feel my eyes, and the only reason I was still surrounded by darkness was because they were shut. I forced my lids open, exerting more effort than I'd ever remembered before, and waited for my eyes to adjust to what was thankfully low lighting.

As my pupils dilated and my eyes worked to snap the wet blurs into sharp-edged objects, I expected to be looking up at the stained ceiling of my apartment. Instead of seeing the explosion of spider-webbing cracks through yellowed plaster, I found myself staring up at a gigantic white bat hanging upside down from the ceiling of what appeared to be a cave. I sat up and pain surged up my midsection, but I ignored it and used my arms to pull myself back away from the creature. When my back met the jagged stone wall, I put my hands up in front of my face, figuring it was too late to try and stand. If I was about to be eaten by a bat-monster I at least didn't want to see it coming.

I waited for death a second time, but it didn't come. I didn't realize I had inadvertently shut my eyes until an uncomfortable amount of silence passed, prompting me to open them. The first thing I noticed was my hands were actually more like claws, which is what made me flinch again, thinking I was being attacked, until I realized the claws were connected to me. They were massive, razor sharp, and while clearly marred with use, they shone like the polished stone of a sculpture. I clutched and unclutched the claws, getting used to the idea they were mine, and followed the slate color of my new hands all the way up muscled arms that appeared to be made from the same polished stone as the claws.

I suddenly remembered the bat and forgot about the foreign body I was occupying. I was far enough back to take in the entirety of the thing and see just how massive it was. Only a few feet were left between the ground and its head as it hung from at least thirty feet above. The only thing stranger than the bat itself was that it was staying extremely still, not even swaying the slightest bit from its upside down perch. The hideously contorted face I'd seen initially was still equally as hideous, but the snarl was fixed and its eyes stared through me into nothing. I gained control of my breathing, only just noticing how hard I was panting, and willed myself to stand on foreign legs.

The same pain I felt from sitting up stung my legs as I stepped forward, but the pain lessened with each step until it was gone completely as I neared the bat creature. I'm not sure how I didn't notice until I was almost on top of it—possibly because the lion's share of my focus was on the giant thing—but just to the side of it was a pile of shimmering gold shit stacked higher than my new head. I stopped short and studied the bat, making sure it wasn't lulling me into a false sense of security before striking. Satisfied it was indeed crippled by stillness, I approached the glimmering pile. I could feel something emanating off it, but I wasn't sure how to interpret the sensation. Either way, even I could tell there was a powerful energy coming from this golden pile of shit.

I stepped up and moved my face to within inches of the pile and caught a glimpse of my new face in one of the smooth, convex, golden surfaces. It was featureless for the most part and resembled more of a stone mask than a face. My eyes were blackened slits gouged into a slick, dark gray surface. I had no mouth—that was for sure—and the only thing resembling a nose were two slits similar to my eyes, only vertical and in the center of my face. I leaned in further and turned. The reflection showed me two pointed horns curving out and back from either side of my head. I instinctively brought the claw hands up to try and remove this mask, but it became instantly clear there was no mask. This was my face.

I stepped back and caught the entire blown out, distorted reflection in the smooth, convex gold. The body that was now mine appeared to be completely made of black and gray stone and moved like it was the soft, pink flesh I was used to. Craggy points jutted from my shoulders, knees, and wrists like aesthetically pleasing implements of death. I twisted my body to the side and was able to catch a glimpse of two smallish black triangles that could only be wings attached to my back, but being made of the same heavy stone as the rest of me, I wasn't sure if they worked.

I started to feel dizzy and stumbled back away from the golden pile of shit, almost running directly into the horrid giant bat-creature I'd momentarily forgotten about. I caught myself, regained my balance, and cradled my head in my giant stone hands while I waited for my bearings to return. I pulled my hands away from my face and took in the bat's face from my now closer vantage point. Its frozen, half-open snarl allowed enough space for me to see three rows of yellowed, pointy teeth like butcher knives, each one longer than the next. Thick strings of mucus-y drool dripped occasionally from the teeth, to the thing's lips, and down to the ground below, serving as the only motion I could detect. I wanted to reach out and touch the bat, but thought better of it. I wasn't ready for that yet, so instead I turned away from the nightmarish face and saw a small opening on the back wall of the cave.

There was nothing else in this place for me to see and hanging around with a huge bat-monster who may or may not just be sleeping or biding its time before it attacked me didn't seem like the best of ideas, so I headed through the opening. The cavernous tunnel was dark, small, and warm. I couldn't accept that this was real and once I was surrounded by darkness it gave me hope that any minute I would open my eyes and be back in my apartment smoking magic cigarettes with the murder-hungry imp I'd summoned days before. Even as I approached the small circle of light at the end of the tunnel, I still held onto the hope that when I exited the cave I would be myself again and at home.

This was not the case, and when I stepped outside I was firmly gripped with the reality of my situation. This was no dream, and it wasn't even a nightmare because ones this frightening simply didn't exist. The sky was fiery red, and four black moons were situated along the horizon. The first of the four hung lower as it began to set behind the sharp cliffs of a mountain range blacker than I thought black could be. The ground around me was cloaked in a thick, black and gray mist that rolled around my legs like the ocean's incoming tide. I stepped forward cautiously, since my view of the ground was obstructed, and came upon the origin of the mist.

It billowed from three giant holes in the ground. Three giant pits. The mist expelled itself from the massive pits with slow, lazy arrogance to fill the space around the holes for what looked like miles to me. I turned back to face the opening to the cave, trying to decide which was worse: being trapped with a monster where at least I knew what I was getting into, or heading out to explore the dark and foreign landscape around me. Neither was ideal, and I could not discern which was the lesser of two evils.

I figured my situation only had the potential to get worse, although I lacked the ability to imagine how. I turned to face the cave once more before making my decision to not visit the great white bat again. I began to slowly traverse my way through the dense, dark mist to see what lay beyond the pits.

Mephistopheles leaned in close to the bathroom mirror and used a washcloth to polish the tiny white horns that decorated either side of his forehead. They were only visible to him and whoever else he chose to reveal his true form to, but that was no excuse to not keep them presentable. Satisfied with the job, he placed the washcloth on the sink and stayed up close to the mirror to examine his flawless, ivory skin. Not a pore was visible and not a hair was out of place, which was, of course, by design. The old demon took great pride in his appearance, and while some had called his vanity weakness, he saw it only as another level of his fantastic strength.

He stepped back to admire the entirety of his impeccably handsome visage and smiled. He was still wearing the same white suit he donned as a tribute to the society he desperately wished to be a permanent part of, and the brightness of it gave off the impression it was glowing. Since he'd achieved his goal of being permanently integrated into human society he could easily have himself appear with an endless array of fashionable suits from anywhere he pleased, but he chose to stick with his trusty white three-piece. Mephistopheles was arrogant and vain, but even he could respect the trials he'd gone through to obtain access to his new residency, and he didn't plan on forgetting about it.

He felt truly at home now, never again having to live under the oppressive thumb of the Old Ones and their ancient magic. He'd outsmarted them. He'd beaten them at their own game, and no one could take that away from him. The only addition to Mephistopheles' outfit was hanging around his neck from a chain that shimmered with the same gold as what hung from it. He reached up and held the golden turd medallion between his thumb and forefinger while musing absently about how far he'd come. The medallion held a great deal of power that Mephistopheles always felt; a power he had complete control over.

The reflection of a beautiful, dark haired woman with eyes that smoldered blackness and a smile that telegraphed mischief appeared in the mirror behind Mephistopheles. He turned on his heels to greet the gorgeous creature, mimicking her smile with his own.

"Are you ready, my darling?" asked Elizabeth. "You don't want to be late for your big appointment."

The medallion began to glow and give off a heat Mephistopheles had grown used to and even yearned for.

"Yes I am, my love," he said, leaning in to kiss her lightly on the cheek. "Yes I am."

John Wayne Comunale lives in the third coast land of purple drank known as Houston, Texas. He is a writer for the comedic collective, MicroSatan, and contributes creative non-fiction for the theatrical art group, BooTown. When he's not doing that, he tours with the punk rock disaster: johnwayneisdead. He is the author of *The Porn Star Retirement Plan*, *Charge Land*, and *Aunt Poster*, as well as the writer/illustrator of the comic-zine, *The Afterlife Adventures of johnwayneisdead*. John Wayne is an American actor who died in 1979.

Other Grindhouse Press Titles

#666__*Satanic Summer* by Andersen Prunty

#033__*Home Is Where the Horror Is* by C.V. Hunt

#032__*This Town Needs a Monster* by Andersen Prunty

#031__*The Fetishists* by A.S. Coomer

#030__*Ritualistic Human Sacrifice* by C.V. Hunt

#029__*The Atrocity Vendor* by Nick Cato

#028__*Burn Down the House and Everyone In It* by Zachary T. Owen

#027__*Misery and Death and Everything Depressing* by C.V. Hunt

#026__*Naked Friends* by Justin Grimbol

#025__*Ghost Chant* by Gina Ranalli

#024__*Hearers of the Constant Hum* by William Pauley III

#023__*Hell's Waiting Room* by C.V. Hunt

#022__*Creep House: Horror Stories* by Andersen Prunty

#021__*Other People's Shit* by C.V. Hunt

#020__*The Party Lords* by Justin Grimbol

#019__*Sociopaths In Love* by Andersen Prunty

#018__*The Last Porno Theater* by Nick Cato

#017__*Zombieville* by C.V. Hunt

#016__*Samurai Vs. Robo-Dick* by Steve Lowe

#015__*The Warm Glow of Happy Homes* by Andersen Prunty

#014__*How To Kill Yourself* by C.V. Hunt

#013__*Bury the Children in the Yard: Horror Stories* by Andersen Prunty

#012__*Return to Devil Town (Vampires in Devil Town Book Three)* by Wayne Hixon

#011__*Pray You Die Alone: Horror Stories* by Andersen Prunty

#010__*King of the Perverts* by Steve Lowe

#009__*Sunruined: Horror Stories* by Andersen Prunty

#008__*Bright Black Moon (Vampires in Devil Town Book Two)* by Wayne Hixon

#007__*Hi I'm a Social Disease: Horror Stories* by Andersen Prunty

#006__*A Life On Fire* by Chris Bowsman

#005__*The Sorrow King* by Andersen Prunty

#004__*The Brothers Crunk* by William Pauley III

#003__*The Horribles* by Nathaniel Lambert
#002__*Vampires in Devil Town* by Wayne Hixon
#001__*House of Fallen Trees* by Gina Ranalli
#000__*Morning is Dead* by Andersen Prunty

Made in the USA
Monee, IL
24 December 2021